The Dante Inferno:

Sev's Blackmailed Bride

The Dante Dynasty Series:
Book #1

by

Day Leclaire

USA Today Bestselling Author

Please Note

This is a work of fiction. Names, characters, places, and incidents either are the product of the author's imagination or are used fictitiously, and any resemblance to actual persons, living or dead, business establishments, events or locales is entirely coincidental.

Cover Design by Melyssa Naujoks, 2019

For more information, please visit my website: http://www.DayLeclaire.com

Thank You.

Book Description

Some blazes, once ignited, can't be extinguished. Just one burning touch connects a Dante with his soul mate. The Inferno ... curse or blessing?

One scorching touch connects Sev Dante with lovely jewelry designer, Francesca Sommers. One passionate night together changes their lives forever. One painful secret will tear them apart and destroy both their lives.

As the powerful, take-charge CEO of Dantes jewelry empire, Sev never believed in The Inferno until it sweeps through him like wildfire. According to family legend, to ignore The Inferno guarantees disaster. To succumb, a life of bliss. But what happens when the woman The Inferno chooses works for his competitor and creates a stunning jewelry collection that threatens to destroy his plans to rebuild his family's empire? The only option available: blackmail her to work for him and become his bride.

Francesca Sommers has her dream job, working for her father, even if he's unaware of her existence. Her life is almost perfect ... until Sev changes her with a single touch. She can't resist him or his relentless seduction. Has no choice but to surrender to his raw passion. To give him everything and anything he demands. Even to be forced into marriage.

But surrendering to Sev means losing both her budding relationship with her father and her career. And when Sev discovers what she did to even the scales and protect her father's business from his hostile takeover, she will lose him, too.

Will The Inferno be enough to save them? Or will its relentless fire consume them both?

Dedication

To my own soul mate, Frank, with much love for your constant patience, encouragement and sense of humor. It just keeps getting better!

Table of Contents

Other Titles by Day Leclaire

The Dante Inferno:

The Dante Dynasty Series

Some blazes, once ignited, can't be extinguished. Just one burning touch connects a Dante with his soul mate.
The Inferno ... curse or blessing?

Prologue

He refused to lose.

He refused to allow anything—or anyone—to get in the way of his rebuilding Dantes into the formidable empire it had once been.

Severo Dante fought for the calm control that typified his business dealings as he regarded his brothers. He found it more difficult than usual to maintain an impassive facade, perhaps because the next few business decisions would prove vital to their overall future. Passion was the hallmark of the Dante name, of the Dante image. But the head of the company couldn't afford to allow emotion to overrule intellect. Too much depended on his ability to handle all that went on behind the scenes.

Where others provided the creativity that turned the sparkle and glitter of gemstones into the world's most coveted wedding rings, Sev utilized logic and business acumen to drag Dantes back from the brink of ruin and propel its return to the public acclaim it had once known. At least, that had been the plan until he hit this latest roadblock.

Sev turned from the panoramic view of downtown San Francisco and faced his brothers. "Timeless Heirlooms was in the perfect position for acquisition. Dantes should already have it tucked beneath our corporate umbrella. What the hell happened?" he demanded.

The Dante twins, Marco and Lazzaro, shrugged as one. "New designer," Marco explained.

"It's revitalized their company," Lazz added.

"Who is this designer? What's his name? Where did he come from?" To Sev's frustration, no one answered. "We need to find out. Now. Timeless Heirlooms belonged to Dantes until we were forced to sell it off after Dad died. Now that I've solidified our financial position, I want TH back. And I want it back *now*."

Marco paced restlessly. "Maybe we should reconsider taking over Timeless. Since we're global again, I'd rather go head-to-head with them and crush them where they stand. We've been cautious long enough. Let's get moving," he persisted. "Expand from our wedding ring market into the areas we once owned—not just heirloom and estate jewelry, but all jewelry needs. Earrings, bracelets, necklaces. Hell, tiaras, if there's a demand for them."

Sev shook his head. "It's too soon. We need a really spectacular collection to launch us, and we don't have that collection, or anything close to one. Nor do we have a suitable marketing campaign, even if one should fall into our laps. By taking over TH we corner that particular market in one simple move. Once solidified there, we'll choose our next target. Something bigger and more impressive." He turned his attention to Lazz. "What's our best approach for finding this new designer?"

"TH is having a spring showing—" Lazz checked his notes with typical thoroughness "—tomorrow night. The Fontaines will be featuring their latest designs, as well as the creative geniuses behind them. One of them has created quite a buzz. Once we have the designer's name, we can order a background check. Find his or her vulnerability."

A cunning gleam appeared in Marco's eyes. "Better yet, we can hire him out from under the Fontaines. He'd make a fine addition to Dantes. Then when we've bought out Timeless Heirlooms, he can go right back to what he's doing now—designing contemporary pieces with the look and feel of heirloom and estate jewelry." A hint of ruthlessness colored his words. "Only he'll do it for TH's new owners. *Us.*"

"That's a distinct possibility." Sev considered his options before reaching a decision. "Here's what I want. It might look suspicious if we all attend TH's show. Lazz, you handle the background check and give us something to go on. Marco, you're the people person. You and I will attend the showing. I'll speak to the Fontaines directly."

Marco smiled. "While I use my natural charm and sex appeal to get the latest gossip."

Lazz groaned. "The worst part is . . . he's right. I've never understood how we can look exactly alike and yet women who won't give me the time of day are all over Marco."

A knock sounded at the door, interrupting a discussion that had been ongoing since the twins had crawled out of their respective cradles. Their youngest brother, Nicolò, walked in. Long considered the family "trouble-shooter," he took charge when creative answers were needed to sort out a family dilemma. Nicolò often claimed that he didn't believe in problems, only solutions.

"Primo sent me," Nicolò said, referring to their grandfather. "He thought you might have a job for me."

Sev nodded. "I want you working with Lazz. He'll fill you in on the latest developments with Timeless Heirlooms. We may need some innovative suggestions in the near future."

Nicolò inclined his head, his expression reflecting both his interest and his fierce determination. "I'll get right on it."

Sev folded his arms across his chest. "When Dad died and we discovered that Dantes teetered on the verge of bankruptcy, we were faced with some unpleasant choices—"

"You were faced," Lazz interrupted. "You were the one forced to make the tough decisions and sell off all the various subsidiaries of Dantes."

"Selling off the secondary holdings saved the core business and allowed us time to recover and rebuild." Sev eyed each brother in turn. "It's been a long road back, but now we're in a position to reclaim what we once lost. I won't allow anything to stand in the way of doing that. We all agreed that the first business we return to the fold is the heirloom and estate jewelry. That's Timeless Heirlooms. If this new designer is all that stands between us and reacquiring TH, then we either find a way to take them over . . ." His expression fell into merciless lines. "Or take them out."

Chapter One

Francesca Sommers ran a critical eye over the sumptuous ballroom in Nob Hill's exclusive five-star hotel, Le Premier, and struggled to suppress a severe case of nerves. In a little over twenty-four hours she'd have her very first showing. She couldn't believe her good fortune, both in being offered the opportunity to work with Tina and Kurt Fontaine, as well as having her designs among those featured at Timeless Heirlooms' spring show.

As though sensing Francesca's nervousness, Tina came up beside her and slipped an arm around her waist. "You can stop worrying right now," she said. "You'll see. Your pieces will be the hit of the evening. Not to take anything away from Cliff or Deborah's talent and skill—they're both good designers—it's your collection that will take everyone's breath away. It offers the perfect blend of romantic elegance and timeless appeal that are hallmarks of my company."

Francesca relaxed ever so slightly, smiling in delight at the compliment. "Are you sure you don't mean old-fashioned?" she asked with a laugh.

Tina lifted a dark eyebrow, which gave her exotic features an imperious cast. "Period pieces are a Fontaine specialty. We're at the leading edge of the resurgence in popularity for jewelry like this. You'll see. Tomorrow night's showing will put us over the top."

Francesca shook her head. "Catching Juliet Bloom's eye will put us over the top. I don't suppose she's responded to our invitation?"

"Her agent contacted us. She's still out of the country wrapping her latest film. But her agency's sending a representative. And I've learned that Juliet's next movie is another period piece. If this rep likes what she sees . . ." Tina lifted a shoulder. "We've all done the best we can. The rest is up to fate, as well as those stunning pieces you've designed."

Kurt entered the room and Tina murmured an excuse before joining her husband. Francesca pretended to give her full attention to the various displays currently under construction, but in reality, she studied her employers with an intense yearning.

As the brilliant and creative owner of Timeless Heirlooms, Tina couldn't be more different from her husband of nearly thirty years. Small, dark, and vivacious, she hurtled through her days, whereas Kurt took life in stride. He also qualified as one of the most strikingly handsome men Francesca had ever met, towering over Tina, his Nordic appearance the polar opposite of his wife's.

Although he held the title of Director of Operations for TH, his real job consisted of supporting Tina and keeping the nuts and bolts of the business end of the company running smoothly. With his calm, reassuring demeanor, he excelled at both, even during stressful and frantic periods such as this.

Francesca gripped her hands together. Right now, Timeless Heirlooms desperately needed Kurt's soothing touch. Despite the Fontaines' attempts to keep everyone in the dark, rumors had reached Francesca of their financial difficulties. They were counting on her—or rather, her designs—to help them recover their footing in the volatile world of jewelry sales. In response, she'd thrown herself, heart and soul, into her job, giving the Fontaines every ounce of her talent and skill. But would that be enough?

For as long as Francesca could remember, she'd wanted to work for one of Dantes' subsidiaries, mainly because it offered an unparalleled opportunity to advance her career and bring her designs to life. But when the Fontaines bought out TH, a far different reason drew her to apply to them for a job, instead of

Dantes. A reason she kept tucked close to her heart.

It gave her the opportunity to get to know her father.

Sev's plans for the evening of the Fontaines' show seemed perfect, right up until he saw her.

For some inexplicable reason, she drew his gaze the moment he walked into the ballroom and the impact from that one look struck with all the power and sizzle of a lightning bolt flung from on high. Every business plan, every thought about taking over TH, of tracking down this new designer and acquiring him for Dantes, leaked from Sev's brain and puddled at his feet. In its place one imperative remained.

Get. The. Woman.

She stood in the midst of a group of people, a tall, golden swan surrounded by sparrows. Everything about her spoke of old-time grace and elegance, the very embodiment of Timeless Heirlooms' motto—jewelry that mates past with present. He knew many beautiful women, but something about this one captivated him on a visceral level. Unremitting desire entangled him in an unbreakable web and refused to let go no matter how hard he struggled to break the bond.

For a split second Sev forgot why he'd come or what he hoped to accomplish. Instead, he felt compelled to follow that primal tug. He would have, too, if Marco hadn't grabbed his arm.

"Hey, where are you going? The Fontaines are in the other direction." He glanced toward the section of the room that held Sev's attention and grinned in sudden understanding. *"Bella, yes?"*

"Yes." The single word—one riddled with desire—betrayed him and Sev shook his head in an effort to clear it. What the hell was happening to him? He never lost focus like this. Nothing ever came between him and business. Nothing. Not even a drop-dead gorgeous woman whose very presence sang with all the promise and allure of a Greek Siren.

Marco straightened his suit jacket. "Since my assignment is to mingle with the guests while you see what information the Fontaines are willing to cough up, I believe the lady in question is on my list." He clapped his brother on the back. "Looks like you're out of luck, Sev."

The mere thought of his brother getting anywhere close to this particular woman had Sev seeing red. Marco, the charmer. Marco, who could entice any and all women into his bed with a single look. Marco, who had never met a woman he hadn't enjoyed to the fullest, before discarding. Marco, with his golden swan.

A faint roaring filled Sev's ears, a noise that deafened him to everything but one increasingly urgent demand. *Get. The. Woman.* "Not her," he ordered. It amazed him that he could still speak coherently, considering the compulsion that infected him and drove him to react in ways in complete and utter contrast to his normal character. "Stay away from her."

Marco still didn't get it. "You're not playing fair," he protested. "Why don't we let the lady decide who she prefers?"

Sev simply turned and looked at his brother. "Not her," he repeated.

Marco held up his hands, the humor fading from his expression. "Fine, fine. But if she approaches me, I'm not sending her away. Not even for you."

Sev's hands collapsed into fists and it took every ounce of effort to keep from using one of them to rearrange Marco's features, arresting features that attracted women to him with lifelong ease, not to mention unparalleled success. "If she approaches you, send her over to me."

Marco frowned. "Have you met this woman before? Do you have a history with her? You know I don't poach my brothers' women. Not unless your relationship's over." His smile glimmered again. "I don't suppose it's over by any chance?"

"It's not over. In fact, it hasn't started. Yet." His gaze fixed on his quarry. "I'm just staking my claim. Now are we clear, or do I have to spell it out with my fists?"

"No, it's not clear. Stake your claim? Spell it out with fists?" Marco's frown deepened. "Have you lost your mind? When have you ever spoken about a woman like that? What's gotten into you?"

Sev drew in a slow breath, fighting to clear his head, with only limited success. What *had* gotten into him? Marco was right. He never reacted like this over a woman. Nothing and no one came ahead of business. But another glance in the blonde's direction caused the desire to erupt in messy waves of molten heat. It filled him with a whispered demand to go to her. To seduce her. To take her and make her his, no matter who or what stood in his way. It overshadowed all else, rooting into his very soul and sending out powerful tentacles that latched on to every part of him and refused to let go.

"Hey! Wake up, big brother." Marco snapped his fingers in front of Sev's nose, concern bleeding into his voice and expression. "I'll tell you what. Why don't we check out the new designs before we get to work? See what we're up against."

"Good idea," Sev managed to say.

Despite the arm his brother dropped on Sev's shoulder, it took every ounce of self-control at his command to turn his back on the blonde and walk away. With every step, he could feel the quicksand of need sucking at his feet and legs. It didn't matter how much distance he put between them, he could still sense her on every level, and that awareness unsettled him more than he cared to admit.

They found the spring collection staged on sweeps of raw silk and took their time studying the pieces. Models also roamed the ballroom, their beauty enhanced by the glitter of diamonds and colored gems. Marco flirted with the models, while Sev assessed the displays. He kept hoping the blonde might gravitate this way. Since she wore one of the premier sets, he assumed she must be a model, as well, especially with her height and regal bearing. But she kept her distance and he couldn't decide whether to be relieved or annoyed.

Marco ended his conversation with a leggy redhead wearing a solid three million dollars' worth of high-quality stones and returned to Sev's side. "I don't get it. Nothing I've seen so far is enough to save Timeless from going under," he said in an undertone. "It's all the same old thing."

"No, not all of it. Not this, for instance."

Sev paused by a display unique in its simplicity. Not that the jewelry needed a fancy backdrop to make it stand out. The pieces spoke for themselves. White gold, diamonds and jet formed a sweeping pattern as elegant and sophisticated as any in recent memory. And yet, an air of romance permeated each item, a promise that by gifting this necklace, or this ring, or this bracelet, the recipient would receive a tangible expression of utter love and devotion.

An image of the blonde wearing the gems flashed through his mind. He could see the delicate strands of the necklace encircling her throat, the graceful length accentuated by the simple drop earrings. It would look perfect on her, particularly when complemented by acres of pale, creamy skin and a simple black silk sheath.

"Aw, hell. This is the first I've seen of this designer's work. It's just the sort of collection I had in mind for Dantes' expansion," Marco said. "We are so screwed."

In more ways than one. If Sev didn't get his mind back on business, he might as well kiss Timeless Heirlooms goodbye. "Find out who designed these and get the information to Lazz and Nicolò," he instructed his brother. "I'll go talk to the Fontaines. Maybe I'll learn something helpful."

Or maybe he should head for the kitchen, grab a bucket of ice and pour it over his head in the hope of dousing the heat rampaging through his system. Damn it to hell! What had that blonde done to him and how had she done it?

Marco grimaced. "Whatever you learn better be helpful, because I have a feeling they no longer need to sell TH."

Unfortunately, Sev had a nasty feeling his brother was right. Still, his conversation with the Fontaines elicited a few interesting facts. They had, indeed, hired three new designers for the express purpose of revitalizing TH. And they had some big deal in the offing, all very hush-hush. Whatever the deal, the Fontaines were convinced it would catapult them into the big times.

Yet, Sev caught the hint of desperation Tina couldn't quite conceal, which told him all he needed to know. Despite tonight's success, they were still vulnerable. He just needed to uncover the source of that vulnerability and exploit it.

He headed for the far end of the room where French doors opened onto a shadowed balcony with a stunning view of San Francisco. The light breeze held a final nip of winter's chill, but he found it a welcome relief after the perfumed warmth of the ballroom. Removing his cell phone from his jacket pocket and hit a button to connect with Lazz.

A few seconds later the call went through. "Sev?" A rapid clicking bled through the line, indicating his brother was typing as he spoke. Ever the multitasker. "I just spoke to Marco."

"And?"

Lazz sighed. "You're both at the same party. So why am I the one keeping you two up-to-date?"

"Do I really need to answer that?"

"Okay, okay. Marco has two names for you so far. There's a Clifton Paris and a Deborah Leighton. He's working on the third one, but everyone's being very mysterious. He thinks it's because they're planning some huge announcement in regard to this final designer."

"Which means he's the one we're after."

"Probably. Marco said there's some special deal TH is about to close, also involving this particular designer."

"The Fontaines said the same thing. Does Marco know what the deal is or which designer?"

"Actually, he does, at least in part. They're about to sign a big-name actress."

Sev fought for patience. "There's a lot of big-name actresses out there. Which one are we looking at?"

"Don't know, yet. But the rumor is, she's at the very top. If they do sign someone like Julia Roberts or Jennifer Lawrence or Juliet Bloom, it'll be huge for them. And it'll effectively prevent both a buyout and, quite possibly, our ability to compete with them on the open market."

Sev grimaced at his brother's all-too-accurate assessment. "I need to find out who they're courting and get the agreement delayed. Put Nicolò on it."

"Right away."

"We also need leverage. Call that PI we hired last year—Rufio—and have him start an immediate investigation of the designers Marco's already identified. Then call Marco and tell him I want that third name ASAP. Tell him to alert me the minute he has it."

"Check."

Sev pocketed his phone. Time to gather himself for round two. He glanced toward the glow of lights, where the subdued chatter of voices wafted from the ballroom. To his relief, his reaction to the blonde had eased somewhat. Five minutes and counting without a single image of her short-circuiting his brain and sending the rest of him into overdrive.

Or so he thought until she appeared in the doorway and stared straight at him. For a split second he believed she came in search of him, that the ever-tightening tendrils between them were acting on a subliminal level and drawing her to him. Then he realized that her eyes hadn't adjusted to the darkness that cloaked him. He nearly groaned. She couldn't see him at all. Did she even sense him? Doubtful. This was his insanity, not hers.

She hesitated while light streamed around her, capturing her in its warm embrace. She'd dressed simply, in a silk sheath of palest lilac. No doubt the color had been selected to complement the jewelry she wore, the set unquestionably the work of TH's mystery designer. A delicate rope of silver, studded with the unmistakable glitter of diamonds and Verdonian amethysts, hugged the base of her neck while a simple confection of the same stones flashed discreetly on the lobes of her ears. Understated. Stylish. Sophisticated.

With a sigh of relief, she stepped onto the balcony. The light from the ballroom gave her a final caress, slipping through the thin silk to reveal a womanly shape that nearly brought Sev to his knees. Full breasts strained against the low-cut bodice, while a nipped waist and shapely hips gave the simple dress an impressive definition.

She crossed to the balustrade and stared out at the view, absently rubbing her bare arms against the spring chill. Sev found he couldn't move. The rational part of his brain ordered him to return to the gathering and finish the job at hand. But an overwhelming need eclipsed that small voice of sanity. It was as though some primeval part of himself dominated reason and rationale. He'd become a creature of instinct. And instinct demanded that he inhale her very essence and imprint it on his mind and body and soul.

Her instincts must have been as finely tuned as his own, for she lifted her head as though scenting the air. Then, with unerring accuracy, she spun to face him and her gaze collided with his.

"I've been waiting for you," he said.

Francesca froze, every nerve ending sizzling to life in an instinctive fight-or-flight reaction. She couldn't say what alerted her to the man's presence. One second she believed herself alone and in the next heartbeat she sensed him on a purely intuitive level.

She stared at him and the breath hitched from her lungs. He blended into his shroud of shadows so completely that the ebony richness of his hair and suit melted into his surroundings, making him appear part of the night. Only his eyes were at odds with the endless darkness, glittering like antique gold against a palette of black. As though aware of her apprehension, he stepped into a swath of light coming from the ballroom to enable her to get a better look.

His height impressed her. He stood a full two or three inches over six feet with an imposing expanse of shoulders and long, powerful legs. For the first time since childhood, she felt downright petite. Reflected light cut across his features, throwing the patrician lines of his face into sharp relief. Heaven help her. She couldn't remember the last time she'd seen such a gorgeous man.

But something stunned her even more than his appearance—the emotional turmoil he triggered. She'd never responded to a man like this before. Never experienced such an intense, uncontrollable physical reaction. She stood before him, filled with a feminine helplessness utterly foreign to her nature. Desire shook her, the intensity so absolute that she could only stare in bewilderment when he offered his hand.

"You've been waiting for me?" she finally managed to say. "Why?"

"I noticed you when I first arrived and hoped we'd eventually meet. My name's Severo. Sev, for short."

"Francesca Sommers." She took the hand he offered before snatching it back with a startled exclamation. "Good Lord. What was that?"

He appeared equally stunned. "Static electricity?"

She'd felt static electricity before. Who hadn't? In fact, as a child she and the other foster children had often delighted in scuffing their socks on the carpet before chasing through the house in order to shock each other. That brief zap of electricity bore no similarity to this.

She scrubbed her palm across her hip, but after that initial searing of flesh against flesh, the sensation changed. It scored her palm like a brand, though unlike a brand, it didn't hurt. It sank deep into her bones—part tingle combined with a peculiar ticklish itch. She didn't know what to make of it.

"Maybe we should try that again," Sev said.

She took a swift step backward. "Maybe we shouldn't."

His mouth tilted to one side. "I'm sorry. I have no idea how or why that happened. You sure we can't try this again?" He held out his hand. "I promise, if anything bad occurs, I'll keep my distance."

She hesitated for an instant, then reluctantly slipped her hand into his. "So far, so good."

The previous sensation didn't happen again, true. Instead, another one took its place. It felt as though some part of him seeped from his hand to hers and sank into her pores before being lapped up by her veins. It slid deeper with every beat of her heart, imbuing her with his essence. Worse, each beat filled her with forbidden desire.

She fought the sensation, fought to speak naturally. "So, what brings you to the showing, Sev? Are you a buyer?"

"Not exactly, although the set you're wearing is something I wouldn't mind acquiring. May I have a closer look?"

No more than a few feet separated them. The single step he took in her direction shrank that distance to mere inches and magnified her reaction to him. Drawing in a deep breath, she tilted her head to one side so he could get a better look at her design, praying he wouldn't take long so she could escape into the relative safety of the shadows surrounding them. The next instant she found escape the last thing on her mind.

His hand brushed her collarbone as he traced the curve of her necklace with his fingertips, branding her with fire. "Stunning. Absolutely stunning."

On the surface his comment sounded simple enough, yet a heavy, old-world lyricism underscored it, filled with the flavor of foreign climes. She could hear the faint strains of a glorious Italian aria, smell the tart richness of ripening grapes, soak in the heat and humidity of a Tuscan summer.

Unable to help herself, she swayed toward him and whispered his name. His response came in a frantic explosion of movement. He swept her into his arms, locking her against him. Hips and thighs collided, then melded. Hands sought purchase before hers tunneled into the thick waves of his hair and his spread across her hip and spine, flooding her with a heavy liquid warmth. Lips brushed. Once. Twice. Finally, their mouths mated, the fit sheer perfection.

She practically inhaled him, unable to get enough. Not of his taste. Not of his scent. Not of his touch. His hands drifted upward, igniting a path of fire in their wake. The most peculiar awareness filled her as he touched her. Though his caress aroused her, she didn't get the impression his actions were a form of foreplay. Instead, it almost felt as though he were committing the shape and feel of her to memory, imprinting her on his brain.

She pulled back slightly, fighting for breath. "I don't understand any of this. We've only just met. And yet, I can't keep my hands off of you."

"I can't explain it, either." Desire blazed across his face, giving him a taut, hungry appearance. "But, it's happening, and right now that's all that matters. Fortunately, that also makes it easy to fix."

Yes. Thank goodness they could fix this terrifying reaction and make it go away. "Fine. Let's get it taken care of."

He caught her hand in his. "Let's go."

"Go?" She resisted his pull, not that it got her anywhere. He simply towed her along. "Go where?"

"I'll pay for a room here at Le Premier, and we'll spend the night working this out of our systems. Come morning, we go our separate ways, flame extinguished."

Francesca fought to think straight. "This is crazy." Severo, a man she'd met just five minutes ago, had kissed her with a passion she'd never known existed and then casually suggested they book a room at a hotel for a night of mind-blowing sex. He seemed to have missed one vital point. "I don't do one-night stands."

He never even broke stride. "In the normal course of events, neither do I. For you, I'm willing to make an exception."

Under different circumstances she'd have found his comment amusing. Without the warmth generated by his embrace, the cool San Francisco air allowed her to regain an ounce of common sense and she pulled free of his grasp. "Wait. Just wait a minute."

She watched him fight for control. "I'm not sure I have a minute to spare." A swift grin lit his face with unexpected masculine beauty. "Will thirty seconds do?"

She thrust her hands into her hair, destroying the elegant little knot she'd taken such pains to fashion a few short hours ago. There was a reason she couldn't go with him. A really good reason, if only she could bring it to mind. "I can't be with you. I need to get back inside. I—I have obligations." That was it. Obligations. Obligations to . . . She released a silent groan. Why the *hell* couldn't she remember? "I think I'm obligated to do something important."

Sev shot a perplexed glance toward the ballroom. "As am I." His mouth tugged into another charming smile, one she found irresistible. It altered his entire appearance, transforming him from austere man-in-charge, to someone she'd very much like for a lover. "Since you don't know me, you won't appreciate what I'm about to say, but right now, I don't give a damn about obligation or duty or what I should be doing or saying or thinking. Right now, finding the nearest bedroom is all that matters."

"I'm not sure—"

He slid his arms around her, pulling her close, and her hands collided with the powerful expanse of his chest. Everything about him seduced her. The look in his eyes. The deep warmth of his voice. The heated imprint of his body against hers. "Perhaps this will convince you."

He lowered his head once again and captured her mouth with his. Where before his kiss had been slower and more careful, this time the joining was fast and certain and deliciously skillful. He teased her lips apart and then slid inward, initiating a duel that she wished could go on forever.

Her hands slid upward to grip the broad width of his shoulders. She could feel the barely leashed power of him rippling beneath her palms, could sense how tightly he held himself in check. And she found that she wanted to unleash that power and break through those protective safeguards. What would his embrace be like if he weren't holding back? The mere thought had her moaning in anticipation.

He must have heard the small sound because he tensed. A compelling combination of desire and determination poured off him. His kiss deepened as he shifted from enticement to an unmistakable taking. He wanted her, and he expressed that want with each escalating kiss. If they'd been anywhere else, she'd have done something outside her realm of expertise. She'd have surrendered to his seduction and given herself to him right then and there.

She'd never experienced anything that felt so right, not in all her twenty-six years. How could she have doubted? How could she have questioned being with this man? She belonged here in his arms and nowhere else. She wanted what only he could offer. More, she wanted to give him just as much in return. As though sensing the crumbling of her defenses, he lifted his head and stared down at her with dark, compelling eyes.

"Come with me," he insisted, and held out his hand. "Take the chance, Francesca."

How could she refuse him? Without another word of protest, she linked her fingers with his.

Chapter Two

Francesca remembered little of their passage from the balcony to the front desk of the hotel. She existed in a dreamlike bubble, every word and action touched with enchantment. From the moment she put her hand in Sev's, the insanity that invaded her earlier came crashing back with even greater intensity. After he collected a key card and made a brief stop at the gift shop for supplies, he led her to a private elevator that whisked them straight to the penthouse suite. It wasn't until she stepped inside that a modicum of common sense prevailed.

"Perhaps we could have a drink and get to know each other," she suggested. "Take this a little slower."

To her surprise, he didn't argue. Maybe he felt the same way she did, overwhelmed and off-kilter. Desperate to regain his footing in this strange new land they'd stumbled upon.

"Let me see what they have in stock." He checked the selection of wines and chuckled, the deep, rich sound tripping along her nerve endings. He hefted one of the bottles. "Well, would you look at this. Here's something you might enjoy. They actually carry one of my family's labels from Italy."

"You're vintners?" she asked in surprise.

"My extended family is." He smiled, the relaxed warmth and humor causing her system to react in the most peculiar way. "I have a huge extended family. You probably couldn't mention a single field of interest where I couldn't find one of my relatives in that business."

"Even the jewelry business?" she joked. Since he'd been at Timeless Heirlooms' showing, he must have some connection to the jewelry industry.

He gave her an odd look. "Especially the jewelry business."

Before she could ask the next logical question—why he'd been present at the showing—he handed her the wine. Their fingers brushed and she caught her breath, the sound a sharp, urgent reaction to his touch. The fragile glass trembled in her grasp and without a word she set it on the closest surface. Slowly, ever so slowly, her gaze shifted to meet his and time froze.

How was this possible? How could she experience such intense feelings for a man she knew nothing about? She'd always kept herself guarded, had made a point to develop previous relationships slowly and with great care. Emotional distance promised safety. This—whatever this was—promised excitement, yet threatened danger.

Spending the night with Sev would change her, mark her in some indelible fashion. And yet, even knowing all that, an uncontrollable yearning built within, sweeping relentlessly through her, a yearning she had no more power to resist than the tide could fight the forces that drove each wave toward shore.

She gave up the battle. Stepping into his arms, she surrendered to his embrace. Relief surged through her, catching her by surprise. It took an instant to identify the cause and realize that it felt wrong to be apart from him, that on some level she needed to touch him and have him touch her. That without him she felt adrift and incomplete.

Without a word, she helped him remove his suit jacket, the heavy silence broken only by the sigh of silk. His tie followed. She tackled the buttons of his shirt next. It felt so peculiar to stand before him and perform such an intimate, domestic chore. This should be a wife's pleasure. Or a lover's. She was neither. Or did a one-night stand qualify her as his lover?

Day Leclaire

His shirt parted, the crisp white of fine cotton juxtaposed against the tawny darkness of his skin. Her hands hovered for an instant, creating an additional contrast of cream against rich gold, before she flattened her palms against hard, bare flesh. She splayed her fingers across the rippled warmth and slid them upward, sweeping his shirt from his shoulders. Desire hummed through her veins and reverberated in her soft murmur of delight.

"Nice," she whispered.

"I plan to make it nicer."

A laugh escaped her. "I didn't notice before, but you have an accent."

His mouth curved to one side, an answering laugh turning his eyes to a dazzling gold. "Maybe it's because Italian was our first language, even though my brothers and I were born and raised in San Francisco."

She wanted to ask more questions, to learn everything possible about him. But more urgent demands took precedence. Unable to help herself, she feathered a line of kisses along the firm sweep of his jaw. It wasn't enough. Not nearly enough. Forking her hands into his crisp, dark hair she drew his head downward and found his mouth with hers.

With a moan of pleasure, she sank inward, tasting the single sip of wine he'd consumed before passion had overruled social niceties. He teased her with a series of gentle kisses, at distinct odds with the ones they had shared earlier.

These tempted. Suggested. Offered a dazzling promise of hot, sultry nights and endless pleasure. She pressed closer, her silk-covered breasts warm and heavy against the bare expanse of his chest. She reached for the zip to his trousers just as an insistent burr came from the cell phone he'd tucked into his pocket. Startled, she took a hasty step back.

"Wait." Sev fished out the phone and set it for voice mail before tossing it toward a nearby coffee table. It missed, clattering to the floor. "There. All taken care of."

"Don't you need to get that?" she asked.

"It's just my brother. It can wait until morning."

A slight frown creased his brow. Once upon a time he'd have taken Marco's call regardless of the circumstances. On some level he recognized the urgency of speaking to his brother. But that urgency faded to a dull, nagging sensation, one easily dismissed.

Nothing like this had ever happened to him before. Not this crazed need. Not taking time away from business for a sexual interlude. Not the haste and desperation of making this woman his. From the minute they kissed, nothing else existed for him but a raw, desperate wanting, one he intended to satisfy.

"Forget about the phone." He cupped her neck and urged her closer, forking his fingers into her hair and tumbling the loosened strands into total disarray. "Forget about everything but right here and right now."

She relaxed against him and in the muted light her hair gleamed softly while her dark eyes held mysteries he longed to probe. He found the zip to her dress and lowered it the length of her spine. She released a sigh as the fabric parted. Inch by inch, the silk slid from her shoulders, revealing acres of smooth, pale skin. It skimmed her breasts before drifting downward to cling to her hips. A simple nudge sent the gown floating to the carpet, leaving her standing within his embrace wearing nothing but garter and stockings, panties and heels. And her jewelry. It glittered against a palate of cream.

He cupped her hips, supporting her as he sank downward, brushing a series of slow, openmouthed kisses from the pearled tips of her breasts to her soft belly. He slipped her heels from her feet and tossed them aside. Then he turned his attention to her stockings. It only took a moment to release the light-as-air nylons and roll them down the endless length of her legs, before disposing of her garter belt.

Damn, but she was sheer perfection, with narrow, coltish ankles, shapely calves and long, toned thighs. He paused where lilac silk acted as her final bastion of defense to press a kiss against the very heart of her. She trembled beneath his touch, sagging within his grasp.

"No more," she gasped. "I mean—"

"I know what you mean," he replied roughly.

And he did. If they didn't find the bedroom soon, they weren't going to make it there at all. He rose and her hands flew to his waistband, ripping at his belt and zipper. He backed her toward the bedroom as she fought to strip him, all the while snatching greedy, biting kisses. In the hallway, he kicked off his shoes and stepped free of his trousers. And then he swung her into his arms.

Sev reached the bed in three short steps and returned her to her feet. He cupped her face, his hands sweeping past the necklace she still wore. The feel of cool gemstones against his heated flesh allowed sanity to return for a brief instant, at least long enough for him to recognize his obligation to protect her jewelry from harm. With a practiced flick of his fingers, he removed necklace, bracelet and earrings and arranged them with due care on the nightstand table.

Satisfied, he returned his attention to Francesca, lowering her to the mattress. She lay in a tumble of creamy white against the darkness of the duvet. Opening the box he'd purchased at the gift store, he removed protection and put it within easy reach. Then he stripped off his boxers and joined Francesca on the bed. Lights from the city drifted through the unshaded windows opposite them, tinting her with an opalescent glow that battled the shadows attempting to conceal her from him.

The peaks of her naked breasts reflected the muted light, while darkness flung a protective arm low across her belly where her final scrap of clothing remained. She lay quietly beneath his scrutiny, her face turned toward his. Light and shadow worked its magic there, as well, the moon slicing a band of brightness across the ripe fullness of her bee-stung mouth, leaving her eyes—eyes the deep, rich brown of bittersweet chocolate—hidden from him.

He traced a path from moonlight to shadow, delving into the mysteries the dark kept hidden. Her eyes fluttered shut and filled him with an intense curiosity to know all she fought to hide. "What are you thinking?" he asked.

"I'm wondering how I came to be here." She shuddered beneath his touch and it took her a minute to finish. "One instant my life is simple and clear-cut and the next it has me so confused I can't think straight."

"Then don't think. Just feel."

He kissed her cupid's mouth. Unable to resist, he captured the plump bottom lip between his teeth and tugged ever so gently. His reward came in the low, helpless moan that escaped her.

"Do that again," she urged.

"All night long, if that's what you want."

He teased her lips once more, light, brushing strokes that promised without satisfying, suggested without delivering. To his amusement, she chased his wandering mouth in greedy pursuit. He finally let her catch him, delighting in the way she coaxed him into a deeper kiss. She gave both promise and satisfaction, delivering on all he'd suggested. He couldn't get enough of the taste of her, of the incredible parry and slide and nibble of lips and tongue and teeth.

With each exchange, the fever within burned higher and brighter, demanding instant gratification. Sev resisted, refusing to rush. Francesca deserved more. For that matter, so did he. He wanted to explore every inch of her, to delve over each luscious hill and into every valley. To commit her to memory, and then repeat the process in case he'd missed something.

"Why have you stopped?" The question came in a whisper, her confusion communicated through the growing tension in her shoulders and back. "Is something wrong?"

"I haven't stopped," he reassured. "I've just slowed down."

"Oh, I get it. You want to drive me crazy."

He chuckled. "Drive us both crazy."

Her tension changed in tenor, no longer a self-conscious nervousness, but a woman's driving desire, full-bodied and certain. A vibrating need sent a burst of urgency through him. Maybe he'd been kidding himself. Slow was guaranteed to kill him.

Her long graceful hands swept across his torso from shoulder to hip, exploring with open delight. Despite her eagerness, he sensed a tentativeness behind each touch, a newness that spoke of sweet inexperience, right up until her hand closed around him with gentle aggression. Okay, maybe not total inexperience. She found the foil packet he'd set aside for their use and ripped it open, sliding the condom over him with deliberate, torturous strokes. Unable to stand another second, he rolled her under him.

Her body gave as only a woman's body could, accommodating the press and slide of a man's passion. The moonlight shifted, fully baring her to his gaze. High, round breasts tempted his caress, the nipples already ripe and taut with need. He gave them his full attention, each sweep of tongue and hand causing her breath to hitch and her heartbeat to race. Drifting lower, he paused long enough to give due attention to an abdomen that combined the sheen of satin with the softness of down.

And then he eased her panties from her hips. He followed their path with a string of kisses, before drawing the scrap of silk and lace off and allowing it to drift to the floor behind him. With that final garment removed, it left nothing between them but heated air. Neatly cropped honeyed curls shielded the apex of her thighs and he cupped her there, drawing a single finger along the damp cleft, inciting a shudder of desperate yearning.

"It's been a while," she warned. He caught the hint of apprehension she struggled to control. "I haven't—"

He was quick to reassure. "I'll go slow. You can stop me if I do anything you don't like."

"I won't stop you." Her eyes darkened. "I can't."

"I'm relieved to hear it." He swept her loosened hair away from her eyes, the dark blond strands framing the face of an angel. "Slow and easy now, sweetheart. Open for me," he urged. "Let me in."

To his relief, she didn't hesitate. Her thighs parted, lifted, exposing her most private secrets to him. Ever so gently he teased the opening, tracing his thumb across the very center of her pleasure. She tensed, drawn bowstring-taut, and the breath escaped her lungs in a moan of sheer delight. Again he circled and swirled, until he sensed she teetered on the very edge, before he eased between her legs and sank into her.

She fisted around him, hot and slick and tight. He fought for control and a modicum of finesse, while instinct rode him, slashed through him, inciting him to take her hard and fast. To mate. To storm her defenses and shatter them once and for all. But he couldn't hurt her like that. She deserved better. Slowly, ever so slowly, he pressed inward. If she hadn't told him of her previous lover, he'd have sworn she'd come to him untouched.

"Am I hurting you?" The guttural tone of his voice shocked him. He could hear the raw, feral quality of a man teetering on the edge. "Do you want me to stop?"

"No. I need . . ." A rosy flush of want rode her cheekbones, and her expression in the moonlight revealed a vulnerability to him and him alone. She twined her arms and legs around him, her fingernails digging into his back. "More, please."

He didn't require any further encouragement. He drove home with a single powerful thrust. Her cry of astonished delight was everything he could have asked for and then some. She moved with him, finding the rhythm with impressive speed, riding the ferocity of the storm with him. He slid his hands beneath her, cupped her bottom and angled her in order to give her the most pleasure.

The storm intensified, howling through him with each stroke. Rational thought fled before a single inescapable imperative. *Take the woman. Make her his.* Put an indelible stamp on her, one that would bind them together from now through all eternity. She belonged to him now, just as he belonged to her. There was no changing that fact. No going back.

The storm reached its zenith, tearing at him, threatening to rip him apart. Even in the midst of the insanity, even at his most frantic, he remained focused on Francesca. Her needs. Her desires. She anchored him, even as she drove him onward, giving and gifting and surrendering. Her unique feminine perfume, the scent of passion, filled his nostrils. He could feel her approaching her climax and sealed her mouth with his. She arched upward as it hit, and he drank in her cry of ecstasy as though it were the sweetest of wines.

It was his turn after that, his release unlike any he'd ever experienced before. She'd done that to him. For him. With him. She'd marked him in some ineradicable fashion. Given him something uniquely hers to give, something he'd never known with any other woman.

"Oh, my," she murmured long afterward, the breath still hitching from her lungs. "That was . . . unexpected."

"Very." As unexpected as it was unforgettable.

Struggling to catch his own breath, he gathered her up and rolled with her to take the weight from her and transfer it to him. She curled close with a unique feline grace, entangling their limbs into an inescapable knot, part feminine silk, part masculine sinew. Full, round curves cushioned hard angles. With the sweet, gusty sigh of a woman well-satisfied, sleep claimed her.

He lay awake for a long time, holding her close. His palm still itched and burned from that first contact and he longed to rub it. He resisted, not wanting to disturb Francesca's slumber.

Their joining should have fulfilled him, satiated whatever fever fired his blood and drove him to make this woman his. It hadn't. Not by a long shot. It should be over now, the flame diminished to a mere flicker. It wasn't. It continued to roar like wildfire driven before a gale. Instead of ending things, their lovemaking had rooted the bond between them, weaving the fabric of their connection into a tight, inseparable warp and weft.

Whether she knew it yet or not, this night had made her his.

Francesca stirred beneath the benevolent rays of the early morning sunshine.

Lord, she felt incredible. Warm. Relaxed. Happy. She didn't know what had caused such an amazing sensation, but considering how fleeting such feelings could be, she didn't want to move in case it went away.

A heavy masculine hand skated down the length of her spine to cup her bottom, giving it a loving pat. "Mmm. Nice."

What the hell? Francesca's eyes flew open and she stared in horror at the gorgeous male relaxing inches from her nose. Sunlight marched boldly across the bed and openly caressed a man whose bone structure managed to combine both a masculine hardness and a mouth-watering allure. Thick, ebony hair framed high, sweeping cheekbones and an aristocratic nose. He smiled drowsily, his wide sensuous lips stirring images of all the places that mouth had been. Memory crashed down on her, overwhelming in its intensity.

What had she done? A better question might have been, what *hadn't* she done? In the brief time they'd spent together, they'd made love in every conceivable fashion. Of course, she'd reveled in every minute. Sev had proven an outstanding lover. But the romantic illusion cast by the glittering evening had faded beneath the harsh reality of morning light. She'd had a job to do last night at Le Premier, and instead she'd—

Francesca bolted upright in bed in a flat-out panic. *Her job!* Oh, damn. Damn, damn, *damn!* What had she done? How could she have been so foolish? The Fontaines were going to kill her when she arrived at the office. She scrubbed the heels of her hands across her face.

This was not good. What in the world would she say to them? How could she possibly explain what she'd chosen to do instead of representing Timeless Heirlooms at last night's showing? She needed to get home immediately and call them. But first, she needed to return the jewelry she'd worn last night before Tina went into total meltdown. Assuming she hadn't already.

Francesca thrust a tangle of curls from her face and looked desperately around for a clock, hyperventilating when she read the glowing digits that warned she had precisely half an hour to get to Timeless Heirlooms and explain herself to the Fontaines.

"Where are you going?" Sev asked in a sleep-roughened voice. He snagged her around the waist and tipped her back into his embrace. "I have the perfect way to start our morning." A slow smile built across his face. "Funny thing. It involves staying right here."

She wriggled against him. "No. Please let go. You don't understand."

"Mmm." He reacted to her movements in a way she'd have delighted in only hours before. "That feels good."

"I have to get to work."

His hold tightened, locking them together from abdomen to thigh. Heat exploded, and even knowing she may have destroyed her career thanks to one night of stupidity, desire awoke with a renewed ferocity that left her stunned. How was this possible? She squeezed her eyes shut. Why, oh why, did this temptation have to hit last night of all nights? And why hadn't their time together satisfied the unrelenting hunger that accompanied it?

Well, she knew one thing for certain. If she hesitated even one more second, she wouldn't get out of this bed anytime soon. Taking a deep breath, she planted both hands against his chest—Lord help her, what a chest—and shoved. To her surprise, she succeeded in freeing herself. One minute she lay cocooned in warmth and the next she stood beside the bed, naked, cold, and vaguely self-conscious. Sev lifted onto an elbow and studied her through narrowed, watchful eyes. Tension rippled through him, and a hint of something dangerous and predatory lurked in his expression.

"I have to get to work," she explained. "Assuming, after last night, I still have a job. I made a huge mistake leaving with you."

His tension increased ever so slightly, and he continued to remind her of a watchful panther debating whether or not to take down his prey. "Which was your mistake? Leaving with me?" He tilted his head to one side. "Or leaving with a couple mil worth of the Fontaines' jewelry? I suspect both the Fontaines, as well as your agency, won't be too pleased. If you'd like, I can place a couple of calls and get you off the hook."

Francesca frowned in confusion. "What agency?" she asked, before waving that aside. "Oh, never mind. More to the point, where's the jewelry?"

Sev gestured toward the diamond-and-amethyst pieces glittering on the bedside table. "Relax. Everything's safe and sound, and more importantly, undamaged."

"Thank God."

She scooped up the set with exquisite care. Since she didn't have the jewelry cases on her, she could only think of one safe place to put them, and swiftly fastened the pieces to her neck, wrist, and ears. It wasn't until she finished that she sensed Sev's gaze on her. His hungry look deepened and made her acutely aware that she stood before him wearing nothing but the designs she'd created. Tension filled the room, heating the air between them.

Her job! How could she have forgotten *again?* The thought propelled her to action. She caught a glimpse of lilac panties peeking from beneath the pleated edge of the dust ruffle and snatched them up before exiting the bedroom. To her dismay Sev followed right behind, wearing even less than she.

The instant they hit the living room, Sev's cell phone emitted a faint buzz from the direction of the coffee table. This time he picked it up and answered it. "What?" His gaze flickered in her direction. "Say that name again? You're certain?"

She spared him a swift glance, concerned by the sudden grimness lining his face. "What? What's wrong?"

He closed his phone with a snap and came after her. "Who are you?" he demanded.

She stepped into her panties and looked around for her dress. "I already told you. Francesca Sommers." She spotted her dress heaped in a silken pool a few feet shy of the couch. A vague memory of Sev's tossing it toward the cushioned back came to her. Clearly, he'd missed.

Before she could snatch it up, Sev caught her arm and spun her to face him. "You're not a model. You're Timeless Heirlooms' new designer."

His statement sounded more like an accusation. She carefully disengaged her arm from his grasp and bent to pick up her dress. It was ridiculous to feel self-conscious after the night they'd spent together. But something about the way Sev stared at her caused her to hold the gown tight against her breasts. "I never claimed to be a model. You must have jumped to that conclusion." She frowned. "What difference does it make, anyway?"

"Did the Fontaines put you up to this? Is that why you followed me onto the balcony last night?" The questions came at her, fast and sharp.

She stared at him in utter bewilderment, combined with a bubble of irritation. "I have no idea what you're talking about. All I know is that if I don't report in to work within the next twenty minutes, I won't have a job. Now, do you mind? I'd like to—"

He cut her off with a sweep of his hand. "I'm talking about a TH employee falling into bed with one of the owners of Dantes five minutes after meeting. I'm talking about you using the oldest trick in the book to gain inside information for the Fontaines."

She jerked backward as though slapped. "Dantes? You work for Dantes?"

"Sweetheart, I *own* Dantes."

The connection hit and hit hard. Her dress slipped from between fingers that had gone abruptly boneless. "You're a Dante?"

"Severo Dante. CEO and chairman of the board of Dantes."

"Oh, God." She was so fired. "I thought you were a buyer." She managed to add two and two, despite working with only half a brain. "You were at the showing last night to scope out the competition, weren't you?"

He looked around. Finding his trousers between the living room and the bedroom, he snatched them up and yanked them on. The man who stood before her now bore little resemblance to the one who'd made such passionate love to her only hours before. With the exception of the unbuttoned trousers riding low on his hips, he wore nothing but an endless expanse of bare flesh.

Desire still hummed between them, calling to her with even more strength and power than the night before. And she might have answered that call, too, if he hadn't used that one word, that single, appalling word—*Dantes*—that had her itching to run in the opposite direction as fast as her wobbly legs would take her.

She wriggled back into the dress she'd chosen with such care for her first showing. She didn't bother trying to hand-press the wrinkles. Nothing would salvage this mess other than a trip to the dry cleaner's. But at least now she could face him on an even footing, or at least on a somewhat even footing.

She planted her hands on her hips. "Okay, let's have this out. You think I came on to you last night so I could find out your plans in regard to TH?" she demanded. At his nod, she glared at him. "How about the possibility of your coming on to me so you could get the inside scoop on TH's plans? After all, you're trying to buy out the Fontaines, aren't you?"

He studied her for a long silent moment. "It would seem we have a problem."

"Oh, no, we don't." She found her shoes kicked under the wet bar and shoved her feet into the spiked heels. At the same time, she thrust her fingers through her hair in an attempt to restore order to utter disaster. "It's very simple from here on out. We avoid each other at all costs and we don't mention last night to anyone. *Anyone,*" she stressed. "If I'd known who you were last night, I'd never have taken off with you."

"Liar."

She closed her eyes, forcing herself to admit the painful truth. "Fine. That's a lie. But I wouldn't have gone with you because you're Severo Dante. It would have been despite that fact." She opened her eyes and fought to keep her gaze level and not betray the profound effect he had on her. "I owe the Fontaines more than I can possibly repay. Betraying them with their chief competitor isn't the sort of repayment I had in mind. So, from now on, we're through. Got it?"

He came for her again, closing the distance so that no more than a whisper of space separated them. It would have been so easy to push aside that cushion of air and take another delicious tumble into insanity. Just the mere thought had her body reacting, softening and loosening in anticipation. He was a Dante, she struggled to remind herself. She hadn't realized that fact before, and therefore couldn't blame herself for what happened the previous night. But now that she did know, she had a duty to keep her distance.

He brushed aside a lock of her hair. Just that slight a touch and she came totally unraveled. "It would seem we have a problem," he repeated.

No question about that. "I've been consorting with the enemy." Still consorted. Still wanted to consort. And then consort some more.

He shook his head. "It's a hell of a lot more complicated than that. Whatever this *thing* is between us? It isn't over." He traced his hand along the curve of her cheek, leaving behind a streak of fire. "It's only just begun."

Chapter Three

Severo left Le Premier, stopping at his apartment only long enough to change, before continuing to Sausalito to confront his grandfather about the events of the previous night. He had questions, questions only his grandfather could answer.

"Primo?" he called, stepping through their front door.

Silence greeted him, which meant Nonna was out and he should continue on toward the gated garden behind his grandparents' hillside home if he wanted to find the object of his search. Sev headed for the kitchen at the rear of the house and stepped from the cool dusky interior into a sunlit explosion of scent and color.

Sure enough, he found Primo hard at work on a bed of native Californian wildflowers. Thick gray hair escaped from beneath the brim of a canvas bucket hat and surrounded a noble, craggy face. At Sev's approach, Primo rocked back onto his heels, grunting in pain from the arthritis that had begun to plague him in recent years.

Fierce golden eyes, identical to Sev's own, fixed on him. "Do me a favor." He spoke in his native tongue, his Italian seasoned with the unique flavoring of his Tuscan birthplace. "Grab one of those bags of mulch and bring it over here. My ancient bones will be forever grateful."

Sev did as ordered. Stooping, he split the bag with a pair of gardening shears and set to work beside his grandfather. Memories from his childhood hovered, other days that mirrored this one, days filled with the scent of cool, salt-laden air combined with rich loamy earth. Long, industrious moments passed before Sev spoke.

"I'm in the mood for a story, Primo."

His grandfather's thick brows lifted in surprise. "You have a particular one in mind?"

Sev spread a generous layer of mulch around a bed that combined the striking colors of golden poppies, baby blue eyes, and beach strawberries. "As a matter of fact, I do." He paused in his endeavors. "Tell me what happened when you met Nonna."

"Ah." An odd smile played across the older man's face. "Are you asking out of simple academic interest, or is there a more personal reason behind your sudden interest?"

"Tell me."

Primo released a gruff laugh at the barked demand. "So. It is personal. You have finally felt the burn, have you, *nipote?*"

Sev wiped his brow before fixing his grandfather with an uncompromising stare. "I want to know what the *hell* happened to me and how to make it stop."

"What happened is what your ancestors always called the Dante Inferno," Primo answered simply. "Some consider it a family curse. I have always considered it a family blessing."

The name teased at a far-off memory. No, not a memory. More of a childhood story, carrying a grain of truth amid the more fantastical elements. "Explain."

Primo released his breath in a deep sigh. "Come. The story sits better with a beer in one hand and a cigar in the other."

Brushing plant detritus from his slacks, he stood and led the way into the kitchen. Cool and rustic, huge flagstones decorated the kitchen floor while rough-hewn redwood beams stretched across the twelve-foot plaster ceiling. A large, scarred table, perfect for a substantially sized family, took up one end of the room, while a full complement of the latest appliances filled the other. After washing up, the two men helped themselves to bottles of homemade honey beer and took a seat at the table. Primo produced a pair of cigars. Once they were clipped and lit, he leaned back in his chair and eyed his grandson through an aromatic haze of smoke.

"I did try and warn you," he began.

"You didn't issue a warning. You told us a fairy tale when we were impressionable children. Why would we put credence in something so implausible?"

"It was real. You just chose not to believe. Not to remember."

The quiet words held an unmistakable conviction, one that threw Sev. "So now I'm supposed to accept that you and Nonna took one look at each other and it was love at first sight? A love inspired by this . . . this *Inferno?*"

His grandfather shook his head. "No, youngling."

Youngling? At thirty-four? Sev just barely managed not to roll his eyes. "Then what happened?"

"I took one look at your grandmother and it was *lust* at first sight." He studied the burning tip of his cigar and his voice dropped to a husky whisper. "And then I touched her. That is when The Inferno struck in force. That is when the bond formed, a bond that has lasted our entire lives. Whether you are willing to believe it or not, it is a bond our family has experienced for as long as there have been Dantes."

"Lightning bolts. Love at first sight. Instant attraction." Sev shrugged. "All names for the same spice. How is our story any different from thousands of others? What makes it *The Inferno* versus the simple chemistry most lovers experience?"

Primo took his time responding. When he did, he came at his answer from a tangent. "Your grandmother belonged to another man. Did you know that?" Bittersweet memories stirred in his distinctive eyes. "She was engaged to him."

Aw, hell. "Not good."

"Now that is an understatement if ever I heard one," Primo said dryly, stabbing the tip of his cigar in Sev's direction. The ring drifted between them like the period to an exclamation point. Sev clenched his hand. Or like the ring of itchy fire centered in his palm. "You need to understand that all those years ago an engagement was as much a commitment as marriage vows, at least in our little village. So, we fled the country and came here."

"Have you ever regretted it?" Sev asked gently.

Primo's expression turned fierce, emphasizing the contours of his strong Roman nose and squared jawline. "Never. My only regret is the pain I caused this other man." His mouth compressed and he lifted his beer for a long swallow. "He was *mio amico*. No, not just my friend. My *best* friend. But once The Inferno strikes . . ." He gave the sort of shrug only a true Italian could pull off. "There is nothing that can stop it. Nothing that can come between those who have known the burn. Nothing to douse the insanity but to make that woman yours and keep her by your side while The Inferno burns evermore, never to ebb or douse. She is your soul mate. Your other half. To deny it will bring you nothing but grief, as your father discovered to his great misfortune."

Sev wanted to refute his grandfather's words, to dismiss them as an aging man's fantasy. But he hesitated, reluctant to say anything now that Primo had mentioned Sev's father. And one other fact held him silent. Everything Primo said precisely matched his reactions last night, which created a serious dilemma for him. He had plans for Francesca, plans other than taking her to bed. To restore Dantes to its former glory, he had no choice but to steal her away from the Fontaines.

"When you first saw Nonna—before you touched—what was it like?"

Primo hesitated as he considered and dug bony fingers into his right hand, massaging the palm. Over the years Sev had witnessed the habitual gesture more times than he could count, long ago assuming it resulted from arthritis or some other physical complaint. Now he knew better. Worse, he'd caught himself imitating the movement over the past few hours. Even now he could barely suppress the urge.

A far away expression entered Primo's ancient gaze. "I had been away at university and returned for *mio amico's* engagement party. I cut through a meadow on my way home and there she was, gathering wildflowers."

The mention of wildflowers made Sev think of Primo's garden. As long as he could recall it had overflowed with local flora. "That must have been a sight."

"You have no idea, boy." The long-ago memory dampened his eyes and his voice grew rough with longing. "She crouched beneath an orange tree in full blossom, singing beneath her breath, her hands like little, graceful hummingbirds darting among purple hyacinth and daises and brilliant, red poppies." He moved his own gnarled hands in slow, clumsy imitation. "So young. So young and innocent I thought God would stop the beat of my heart for daring to gaze upon such beauty and virtue."

Sev could see the image as though it moved before him. "Then what?" he demanded.

"The wind whispered to her, sending a shower of orange blossoms raining down on brown ringlets that tumbled all the way to her hips. She wore a thin cotton dress and the afternoon sun shot it full of golden rays, outlining—" Primo broke off abruptly and glared at his grandson. "Never you mind what it outlined, *nipote*. Suffice to say, the minute I set eyes on Nonna, it was as though we were connected. As though a ribbon of desire joined us. The closer we came, the stronger it grew. When we touched, the ribbon became stronger than a steel cable, binding us together so we could no longer distinguish my heartbeat from hers. We have beat as one ever since."

The story affected Sev more than he cared to admit, probably because it rang with such love and adoration and simple sincerity. True or not, Primo clearly believed every word. Not that the origins of his grandparents' romance helped with his current predicament. Okay, so he'd felt that connection, the shock and burn when they'd touched, that ribbon of lust, as he preferred to consider it. But ribbons could be cut.

"How do I get rid of it?" he demanded.

Primo drank down the last of his beer before setting the empty bottle on the table with enough power that the glass rang in protest. "You do not," he stated unequivocally. "Why would you want to?"

"Because she's the wrong woman for me. There are . . . complications."

Primo released a full-bodied laugh. "More complicated than her belonging to your best friend?" He swept his hand through the air, the gesture leaving behind a smoky contrail. "It is impossible to cut the connection. The Inferno has no respect for time or place or complication. It knows. It chooses. And it has done so for as long as there have been Dantes. You either accept the gift and revel in the blessing it offers, or you walk away and suffer the consequences."

Sev stilled. "What consequences?"

"You ignore The Inferno at your own peril, nipote." He leaned forward, each word stone-hard. "If you turn your back on it, you will never know true happiness. Look at what happened to your father."

"You think The Inferno killed him?" Sev demanded on a challenging note. "Are you that superstitious?"

Primo's expression softened. "No, it didn't kill Dominic. But because he chose with his head instead of his heart, because he married your mother instead of the woman chosen for him by The Inferno, he never found true happiness. And both our business and our family suffered as a result." He took a slow drag of his cigar, the tip flaming with an unholy red glow. "I am warning you, Severo Dante. If you follow in your father's footsteps you, too, will know only the curse, never the blessing."

Tina Fontaine threw herself into a chair near where Francesca sat at her drawing board, while Kurt filled the doorway leading into the small office. One look at their expressions warned Francesca that her previous night's indiscretion had left her career teetering on a knife's edge.

"You owe my dear husband a huge thank you for stopping me from calling the police last night," came Tina's opening volley.

Francesca stared in horror. "The police?"

Tina leaned forward, not bothering to disguise her fury. "It was your big night. And you disappeared with a bloody fortune in gems around your neck without bothering to tell anyone where you'd gone. What did you expect me to do?"

Francesca clasped her shaking hands together. "I'm sorry. Truly. I have no idea what came over me."

The ring of truth in Francesca's comment gave Tina pause. "Where the hell did you go?"

"I think I can guess," Kurt inserted. "Holed up somewhere clutching a wastebasket, were you?"

Francesca stared at him, utterly miserable. She didn't have any choice. She couldn't lie. She had to admit the truth and take whatever punishment they chose to dole out, even if it meant the end of her career at TH. "Not exactly. I—"

From behind Tina's back, Kurt gave a warning shake of his head. "But you were suffering from a severe case of nerves, I assume?" Before Francesca could reply, he continued, "It's the one excuse Tina can sympathize with, can't you, darling? It happened to her on the night of her first show, too."

Tina gave an irritable shrug. "Yes, fine. It happened to me when we opened our first jewelry store in Mendocino. Too many nerves, too much champagne, and too little intestinal fortitude." She shot Francesca an annoyed look. "Is that what happened?"

Francesca hesitated, before nodding despite nearly overwhelming guilt. "I'm so sorry. The crowd got to me and I decided to leave early." She kept her gaze fixed on Tina, but caught Kurt's small look of approval. "I promise it won't happen again."

"I suggest it doesn't. Next time I'll fire you." Tina continued to stare with uncomfortable intensity. "How in the world did you evade security? I need to know so in future our designers and models can't pull a similar stunt."

Francesca kept her gaze fixed on her drawing table. "There's an exit off the balcony," she whispered. "One of the guests escorted me."

"Go on."

Francesca swallowed. "As for the jewelry, I can't tell you how sorry I am that I worried you. I swear I kept it safe." Or rather Sev had. She'd been too far gone by that time to give a single thought to what damage their lovemaking might do to the delicate pieces.

"That's the only thing that saved your job," Tina said sternly. "If anything had happened to the jewelry, you'd be cooling your heels in jail."

Tina's assistant appeared before she could say anything further and leaned into the room around Kurt. "Call for you," she informed her boss. "It's Juliet Bloom's rep."

Tina came off the chair as though catapulted and flew toward the door. She paused at the last instant. "Fair warning, Francesca." She threw the admonition over her shoulder. "The rep wasn't happy when I couldn't produce you last night. If she's calling to blow off our deal because you were incapable of doing your job, you're gone."

Francesca fought to draw breath, seeing her career vanish before her eyes thanks to one night of utter foolishness. "I understand."

"And there's a call for you on line three, Francesca," the assistant added, with a hint of sympathy.

"Excuse me for a minute," she murmured to Kurt. She picked up the phone, not in the least surprised to hear Severo Dante's voice respond to her greeting. "How may I help you?" she asked in as businesslike a tone as she could manage.

"Huh." He paused as though giving it serious thought. "I'm not quite sure how to answer that. Most of the possibilities that come to mind would be interesting variations on last night's theme."

She didn't dare respond to the comment. She'd risked quite enough already, thanks to Sev. "I'm really busy right now. Could I get back to you in regard to that?"

"In regard to that, you can get back to me anytime you want. But I'm calling for a different reason, altogether. I want you to meet me for lunch at Fruits de Mer at one."

She spared Kurt a brief, uncomfortable glance. "That's not even remotely possible."

"In hot water, are you?"

"Yes."

"Then let's make it tomorrow."

"I'm sorry, that's quite impossible."

"Make it possible or I'll come by the office and let you explain my presence to the Fontaines. Or better yet, I'll explain everything to them. Personally."

Oh, God. If he did that, she'd be fired for sure. Painfully aware of her father listening in, she chose her words with care. "You are *such* a *gentleman.*" Let him read between those lines, or rather, lies.

He chuckled. "You're not alone, are you?" At her pointed silence, he added, "I'm serious. We need to talk. Will you come tomorrow?"

"It would seem I have no other choice. Now, I really have to go." She ended the conversation by returning the receiver to its cradle. "I'm sorry about that, Kurt."

He regarded her far too acutely. "I assume that was your young man from last night?" He held up a hand before she could reply. "I caught a glimpse of you and your mysterious friend leaving together."

Francesca stiffened in alarm. Had he recognized Sev? No, he couldn't have or he wouldn't be acting so understanding. "And that didn't worry you?" she asked hesitantly.

"Not when I consider some of the antics Tina and I got up to when we were first dating. I do, however, recommend in the future that you don't mix business with pleasure."

Embarrassed color warmed Francesca's cheeks. "I hope you know that I don't usually . . . I'm not—"

He waved that aside, but not before she saw his cheeks turn a ruddier shade than normal. "I helped you out of a tight spot this time because, quite frankly, we need you and what you can do for Timeless Heirlooms. But I won't bail you out again."

"I understand." It killed her to be having this conversation with her father. More than anything she hoped to win both his approval, as well as his friendship. Instead, he'd helped her lie to his wife and put their relationship at odds. "As I told Tina, it won't happen again."

"Listen to me, Francesca." He took the chair Tina had vacated. "Your six-month contract with Timeless Heirlooms is almost up. Tina and I are both very excited with what we've seen from you so far. Equally as important, we've enjoyed working with you."

She smiled in genuine pleasure. Receiving such a huge compliment from her father meant the world to her. "Thank you. I've enjoyed working with you, as well."

How could she not? She was living the dream of a lifetime, one she wanted more than anything. Thanks to the detective she'd hired, she'd been able to track down her father the minute she'd graduated from college and approach him without anyone being the wiser. To her delight, she discovered that he shared her passion. Even more incredible, the company he and Tina ran were actively hiring designers, if only on a trial basis.

"Tina and I were on the verge of making your position here permanent. But after last night, we simply can't take the risk. Not yet. You understand our predicament, don't you?"

Her smile died. In the past six months she'd struggled to prove herself as both a top-notch designer, as well as a woman he'd be proud to claim as his daughter. It had all gone so well. Until last night. And now she'd ruined everything.

"I do understand," she managed to say. "Kurt, I can't thank you and Tina enough for giving me this opportunity. I swear I'll make it up to you."

"I don't doubt that." He offered her a slow, generous smile, one that never failed to fill Francesca with an intense longing. He stood and held out his hand. "We'll give it another couple months. Maybe once we have Juliet Bloom under contract, we'll feel more comfortable offering you a permanent position with us."

Francesca slipped her hand into his bearlike grasp, fighting back tears. Determination filled her. It didn't matter what it took, she'd find a way to win his approval, as well as a permanent job at Timeless Heirlooms. If that meant avoiding Sev—well, after the lunch he'd forced on her—then that's what she'd do. Because nothing was more important than having the opportunity to get to know her father, even if she could never tell him the truth about their relationship.

"Thank you for offering me another chance," she said with as much composure as she could manage. "You won't regret it."

"All right," Francesca stated the minute she joined Sev at Fruits de Mer. She took the seat across from him and folded her arms across her chest. "You blackmailed me into coming here. What do you want?"

Sev studied her silently for a long moment. If he could peg her with a single word it would be defensive. From the moment she'd stepped foot in the restaurant and spotted him, she'd had trouble meeting his gaze. He could guess why. He'd seen this woman naked. Had taken her in his arms and made love to her, not once or twice, but three times during their night together, each occasion more passionate than the last. It should have ensured an ease between them. And maybe it would have, except for one vital detail.

Forty-eight hours ago they'd been total strangers.

And yet, nothing had changed. No. That wasn't true. If anything, the attraction between them had grown, become more palpable. He could see the hunger and desire lurking in the depths of her gaze, unwanted as it was undeniable. Her pulse throbbed in her throat and a heated flush touched her cheeks. Most damning of all, her body reacted to his presence. A heated flush touched her cheeks and her pulse throbbed in her throat. His gaze dipped downward briefly, not surprised to see the hard peak of her nipples against the thin silk of her blouse.

"You expected things to be different," he said. "Didn't you?"

She looked at him, the unremitting darkness of her eyes making a startling contrast to her pale complexion and honey-blond hair. "Today, you mean?" She gave him her full attention, a painful vulnerability lurking in her gaze. "Let's just say I'd hoped things would be different."

She'd changed toward him since their night together and he could guess the reason. Now that she'd discovered his identity, she'd decided to end things between them, something he refused to allow. "You hoped our reaction to each other would change now that you know who I am. Because you work for Timeless Heirlooms and I own Dantes, you thought that fact would put a stop to what we're experiencing."

"Yes." A slight frown creased her brow. With a swift glance toward nearby tables, she dropped her voice to a whisper. "I need to explain something. I don't know who that woman was two nights ago. I've never—" She took a deep breath. "I'm not making excuses."

"Of course not." He understood all too well. "But that doesn't alter the facts."

She retreated from him, icing over tension and longing with such speed he suspected she'd had many years of practice. "As far as I'm concerned, whatever happened between us has run its course."

He tilted his head to one side. "Because you say so? Because it would be so much more convenient on the work front?" He couldn't help laughing. "You're kidding, right? This isn't something you can cut off like a light switch."

"I think it is."

He studied her for a moment to assess her veracity. Satisfied she actually believed the nonsense she trotted out, he placed his hands flat on the table. He slid them across the linen-covered surface, inch by inch. When his hands came to within a foot of hers, she released a soft groan.

"Okay," she said, snatching her hands back. "Point made. Maybe this . . . this—"

"Attraction? Desire?" He lifted an eyebrow. "Lust?"

She waved the choices aside. "Those are just varying shades of the same thing."

"And you're still experiencing each of those shades, as well as every single one in between."

He caught the faint breathy sound of air escaping her lungs. "Whatever this is hasn't run its course at all, has it?" she asked.

"Not even a little." He massaged the tingle in his right palm. "I could feel you, you know."

Her brows shot up. "Feel me? What do you mean?"

"When you walked in the room, I didn't even have to see you," he admitted. "I could feel you."

Her brow wrinkled in confusion. "I don't understand any of this," she confessed. "How is that possible?"

He didn't answer. Couldn't answer. "Is it the same for you? Has it eased off any since that night?"

She wanted to lie, he could read it in the hint of desperation in those huge, defenseless eyes. "Maybe it has." She moistened her lips. "I'm sure it's not quite as bad as the other night. It can't be."

"There's an easy way to tell." He extended his hand across the table once again. "Go ahead. Touch me."

Francesca hesitated for a telling moment before splaying her fingers and linking them with Sev's. She gasped at the contact, going rigid with shock. The next instant everything about her softened and relaxed, sinking into what he could only describe as euphoria. Then the next wave hit. A hot tide of need lapped between them, singeing nerve endings and escalating desire.

"I want you again." He told her precisely how much with a single scorching look. "If anything, I want you even more than last time."

"We can't do this. Not again," Francesca protested. "I've already put my job in jeopardy by spending the night with you. If the Fontaines find out it was you at the show, that you were the reason I left, they'd fire me on the spot. I won't risk that. Working at TH is too important to me."

Didn't she get it? "You want me to stop?" He lifted their joined hands. "Tell me how. Because I'd love to know."

She leaned forward, speaking in a low, rapid voice. "What I want is an explanation. Maybe if I understood how and why, I could make it stop. Why do I feel such an odd sensation every time we join hands? Why does just a touch cause me to go all wonky inside?"

His mouth twitched toward a smile. "Wonky?"

She squeezed her eyes shut. "Hungry. Lusty. Horny as hell. God, I can't even believe I'm saying those things!"

He hesitated, loath to repeat the story Primo had told him. But she deserved some sort of answer, even one as far-fetched as The Inferno. He didn't believe they were experiencing anything to do with something so fantastical. Or that his grandfather's Inferno fairy tale belonged just there, in fairy tales. None of that mattered. Regardless of what he thought, she should know.

He forced himself to release her hands, despite an almost uncontrollable urge to sweep her up in his arms and bolt from the restaurant with her. More than anything he wanted to hole up somewhere with acres of bed, twenty-four-hour room service, and a suitcase full of condoms.

"Look, I think I can explain this, though the explanation is going to sound a bit crazy." Nor was this the venue he'd have chosen to tell a woman about The Inferno. But at least a crowded restaurant would give the illusion of safety once she'd fully ascertained the extent of his family's insanity. He gave it to her straight. "There's a Dante legend that my grandfather swears is true, about an Inferno that occurs when a man from my family touches the woman meant to be his."

Her eyes narrowed, but at least she didn't run screaming from the restaurant. "Somehow I don't think this is the sort of story we should hash out in public. Do you?"

"Not even a little. My place isn't far from here. We can talk there, if you'd prefer."

"Talk?" A swift laugh bubbled free and she regarded him with wry amusement. "That would make a nice change. I don't suppose you can promise that's all we're going to do?"

He shook his head. "I can't promise a thing where you're concerned." He leaned back, giving her enough room to breathe. Hell, giving them both enough room to think straight. "But I swear, I'll try. Will you trust me enough to come with me?"

She turned those bottomless dark eyes on him in silent assessment. He'd never met a woman quite so fascinating. She faced the world with elegance and strength and feminine dignity. And though he sensed they were integral parts of her, he also suspected they were a shield she used to protect herself from hurt.

Every so often he caught a glimpse of a waif peeking out, nose pressed to the glass, the want in her so huge and deep it amazed him that one person could contain it all. And yet, he also saw the steely determination that carried her through a life that—if he correctly read all she struggled to conceal—had slammed her with hardship while offering little joy to compensate.

After giving his offer a moment's thought, she nodded. "I promised to meet you this one last time before we parted company, and I will. Besides, I always did like fairy tales even though they never come true." A tragic smile played about her perfect bow mouth, tempting him beyond measure. Then she surprised him by lifting a hand and signaling the waiter. "But who knows. Maybe this one will be different."

Chapter Four

Ten short minutes later they arrived at his Pacific Heights Georgian residence. "This is your home?" Francesca asked, clearly stunned.

He could tell the size and grandeur unnerved her. Hell, as a child it had unnerved him, as well. Built in the 1920s, his grandparents purchased it during Dantes' heyday, when Primo controlled the reins of the company.

Sev had recently updated the house from top to bottom, taking a diamond in the rough and giving it the glitter and polish it deserved. While still on the formal side, he'd made a point to add a more welcoming feel to the place. From the two-story entry foyer, a curving staircase, complete with wrought-iron railing, swept toward the second story and an endless array of rooms perfect for entertaining.

"When I'm hosting guests, I stay here. More often I use my Nob Hill apartment. It's more compact. More to my taste." Unable to resist touching her, he slid his hand down her spine to the small hollow just above her buttocks and guided her toward the private den he kept exclusively for his own use. "This is my favorite room in the house."

Francesca visibly relaxed as she looked around. Light filtered in from a bank of windows that provided an unfettered view of the bay and Alcatraz Island. Two of the other walls bulged with books that overran the floor-to-ceiling mahogany cases. The final wall, at right angles to the windows, offered a cozy fireplace fronted by the most comfortable couch Sev had ever owned. He used the electronic controls to light the fire and gestured for her to have a seat.

It amused him that she took the precaution to sit as far from him as the couch cushions allowed. Understandable, but still humorous. "Okay, let me give it to you straight," he began.

She listened intently while he ran through Primo's explanation of The Inferno, refraining from asking any questions until he finished speaking. "You said that, in the past, your family experienced this Inferno," she said after a moment. "What about your brothers? Have they felt anything similar?"

"I'm the first," Sev replied.

Wariness crept into her gaze. "That suggests you buy in to all this."

"No, not really." And he didn't, despite Primo's insistence that legend matched reality. "I think it makes for a charming story, but a story, nonetheless."

"Then how would you explain what's happened to us?"

He'd given that a lot of thought and decided to believe the simplest explanation. "It's nothing more than lust. Given time, it'll fade."

Though she took his comment with apparent equanimity, a pulse kicked to life at the base of her throat, betraying her agitation. "But what if it's more than that? Has it ever infected the women in your family?"

"I don't understand. Which women?"

She made an impatient motion with her hands. "Haven't any of the Dante men had daughters? Have any of the Dante women experienced this Inferno?"

Sev shook his head. "There's only been one daughter in more generations than I can recall. My cousin, Gianna. Here, let me show you."

He circled the couch to a cluster of photos on a console table and picked up a panoramic photograph in a plain silver frame that showed a group shot of all the Dantes. Seated in the middle were Nonna and Primo. Sev, his parents, and brothers stood to Primo's right, while his Aunt Elia, and Uncle Alessandro, with their brood of four, stood beside Nonna. He handed the picture to Francesca when she joined him, tapping the image of the only female of his generation, a striking young woman with Sev's coloring.

"If Gia's been cursed by The Inferno, she's never mentioned it."

A hint of laughter lightened Francesca's expression. "Cursed? I thought you said Primo called it a blessing."

He couldn't help himself. He leaned toward her, cupping her cheek. "Does it feel like a blessing to you?"

She shut him out by closing her eyes, concealing her inner thoughts. "No, this isn't a blessing. It's a complication I could live without." She eased back from his touch and opened her eyes again, at the same time slamming impenetrable barriers into place. "And what about the other women? The women who are the object of the Dante men's . . . blessing?"

"Like you and Nonna and Aunt Elia?"

"Yes. What choice do we have? How do we escape this Inferno?"

He gestured toward the image of his parents. "My father escaped by marrying someone else."

Francesca blinked in surprise. "Your mother wasn't an Inferno bride?"

Sev shook his head. "Shortly after they died, I discovered letters that indicated he'd been in love with one of his designers, but married my mother, instead."

"Why didn't he marry the woman he really loved?" she asked hesitantly. "Do you know?"

Sev shrugged. "When I confronted Primo about it, he admitted that my mother had invaluable contacts in the industry. It was more of a business arrangement than a true marriage. Not that it did either of them any good."

"What went wrong?"

Maybe it was the hint of compassion he heard in her voice, but he found himself opening up in way he never had with any other woman. "All of my mother's contacts couldn't make up for my father's lack of business savvy." He studied the photograph. God, they looked so youthful. Just six or seven years older than his own thirty-four, he suddenly realized. They also looked remote and unhappy, though how much of that related to their marriage and how much to business difficulties, he couldn't determine. "They were on the verge of a divorce when they died in a sailing accident."

"And you blame that on The Inferno?" she asked in patent disbelief.

"No. I blame it on bad luck." He couldn't tell her the rest. Couldn't admit that he blamed himself for what happened right before and immediately after his father's death. That piece of guilt he kept locked tightly away. "I'd just graduated from college. The day after their funeral, I stepped into my father's shoes. I spent the first year of my tenure dismantling Dantes and the last decade rebuilding it."

"I'm so sorry." She slipped her hand into his and squeezed. Just that, and yet it made all the difference. The connection between them intensified in some indefinable way. Before it had been sheer sex, or so he believed. Now another emotion crept in, one he resisted analyzing. She hesitated a split second before confessing, "I lost my mother, too. I know how painful that must have been for you."

That might explain some of the sorrow he'd seen lurking in her eyes. "How old were you?" he asked.

"Five." Soft. Abrupt. And a clear message that she had no interest in pursuing the conversation.

Not that he planned to drop it. He'd just approach the subject with more care. "It helped that my brothers and I were older, though at just sixteen, Nicolò had a tough time adapting. Fortunately, Primo and Nonna stepped in, which made a huge difference." He paused.

"What about you? Did your father ever remarry?"

"My parents weren't together," she admitted, avoiding his gaze. "I went into foster care."

Oh, God. He tiptoed across eggshells. "Didn't the authorities contact him?"

"They didn't know who he was. I didn't find out myself until after I'd graduated from college and hired someone to locate him for me." She picked up the next picture in the line, putting a clear end to the discussion. A slight smile eased the strain building around the corners of her mouth. "Primo and Nonna on their wedding day, I assume?"

"They eloped right before immigrating to the U.S."

The ancient black-and-white showed a couple arrayed in wedding finery. They looked impossibly young and nervous, their hands joined in a white-knuckle grip. But the photographer managed to catch them in an unguarded moment, as they gathered themselves for a more formal pose. They glanced at each other, as though for reassurance, and the power of their love practically scorched the film.

"Nonna didn't want to escape The Inferno, did she?"

"No."

Francesca returned the photograph to the table with clear finality. "Well, I do." She paced restlessly toward the windows. Once there, she glanced over her shoulder. With the sunlight at her back, her expression fell into shadow. But he could hear the tension rippling through her voice. "I'm not interested in you or the Dante Inferno or having an affair with you. I just want to be left alone to pursue my career. This is a distraction I don't want or need."

"I wish it were that simple. That I could make it go away for you. But I can't."

He wanted to see her, to look into her eyes and know her thoughts. To touch her and reestablish the physical connection between them. Without conscious thought, he joined her at the windows. The instant he slid his palm across her warm, silken skin, his world righted itself.

"Why can't I just walk away from you and never look back?" she demanded. He heard the turmoil underscoring her question, while hunger battled common sense. And he understood what she felt since it mirrored his own reaction to their predicament. "Why can't I simply return to the life I built for myself?"

"You can. We both can." Steely determination enveloped him. "The minute we work this out of our systems."

Sev swept Francesca up into his arms and carried her to the couch. She murmured a token protest, one lost beneath the series of tiny, biting kisses he scattered along her throat. They tumbled onto cushions that molded to their entwined bodies and enfolded them in a private world of suede-covered down. The buttons of her silk blouse parted beneath his hands, revealing a feminine scrap of lace that struggled to contain her breasts. He couldn't help himself. He reared back, drinking in the sight.

Two nights ago, he'd seen her by moonlight and thought it impossible for her to look any more stunning than adorned in shades of silver and alabaster. But now, with her hair and skin gilded in sunlit gold, she robbed sense and sensibility with her beauty. Inch by inch, he lowered himself onto her. And inch by inch, the heat they generated soared, an inferno in the making. Given the number of promises he'd made and broken, he half expected her to push him away. Instead, she basked in that heat and wrapped him up in an ardent embrace.

It was as though they'd never left off from the night before last. He reacquainted himself with her mouth, plundering inward. She moaned in welcome and met him with a feminine aggression that sent him straight over the edge. There were too many clothes between them. He yanked at his tie and the first few buttons of his shirt, but somehow he'd lost the ability to work past the knot imprisoning him. Instead, he turned his attention to her and unhooked the front clasp of her bra. He filled his hands with her bountiful breasts and her breath escaped in a fevered rush.

"We were supposed to have worked this out of our systems by now," she gasped.

"We will." Maybe in a decade or two. "But until then I need your hands on me. I need to be inside you again."

He shifted a knee between her legs and slid the hem of her skirt upward, uncovering acres of smooth, creamy thigh and a tantalizing glimpse of butter-yellow panties. He itched to explore all that lay beneath that scrap of silk. To see those soft curls gilded with sunlight, as well. He ran a finger along the scalloped edging, stroking inward toward dewy warmth until he found the sweet heart of her.

Francesca groaned in response, a rich, feminine, keening sound that called to him on every level and drove him ever closer to the edge. He knew that sound, had heard her make it countless times during the night they'd spent together. But there was another sound he wanted to hear. Needed to hear. The sound she made when she climaxed in his arms.

She shuddered against his stroking touch and he couldn't stand it another minute. He needed her. Now. In a single swift move, he skimmed her panties down her thighs and tossed them aside. Next, he ripped his belt free and unfastened his trousers, pausing only long enough to remove the protection he'd had the foresight to stick in his pocket before their meeting. Her hands joined his, helping to free him from the restriction of his clothing. And then she cupped him, her touch cool against the burning length of him. Instead of easing the raging fire, it only served to intensify it.

He couldn't remember the last time he'd been so desperate to have a woman that he'd been unable to make it to the comfort of his bedroom. With Francesca, nothing mattered except to have her, right here and now. He lifted her and slid deep inside. Her legs closed around him as she welcomed him home.

His groan of pleasure mingled with hers, the heavy pounding of his heart in perfect tempo with hers. The breath exploded from her and then he heard her siren's song, signaling her scramble toward the highest of peaks. He joined her there, calling to her, mating with her, locking them together until he could no longer tell where her body ended and his began.

They moved in perfect harmony, continuing a dance that had begun their first night together. The tempo this time around quickened, turning fast and hard and greedy. He couldn't get enough of her, not how tightly she clenched around him or how she cushioned him against the softness of her woman's body or how she met each thrust with joyous abandon. Long before he was ready for the encounter to end, she spasmed beneath him, and he found he couldn't hold back, couldn't resist going up and over the peak with her before crashing down the other side, holding her tight within his arms.

Long minutes passed without either of them moving, maybe because movement proved a physical impossibility. Finally, the breath heaving from his lungs, Sev levered himself onto his elbows and gazed down at Francesca.

Heaven help him, but she was beautiful, her face delicately flushed with the ripeness of passion, her mouth moist and swollen from his kisses, her eyes heavy-lidded and slumberous. In that moment, his world rested within the warmth of her grasp. How had she come to mean so much to him in so short a time?

"I can't walk away from you, Francesca." Pure steel swept through the words. "And I won't."

She closed her eyes with a groan. "I shouldn't have agreed to have lunch with you. I should have known we'd end up like this again."

He caught the hint of regret and deliberately kissed it away, plying her with soft caresses and long, slow strokes until she trembled in his arms. "Something tells me we'll always end up like this."

Her eyes flew open, the sultry darkness lit with a want so deep and strong, she couldn't disguise it as anything else. "We can't. We can't do this again," she whispered through lips still red and swollen from his kisses. The scent of their passion enclosed them, belying her statement and he could feel the tension within her battling against the soft, hungry give of her body.

Sev wanted her again. Again and again and again. For the moment, he'd allow her to escape. But only for the moment. He eased himself up and off her. Holding out his hand, he assisted her from the couch and helped return a semblance of order to her clothing.

"I didn't give you a choice about lunch," he informed her. "And just so you know, I don't plan to give you a choice in the future, either."

She eyed him in open alarm, but didn't ask the question he suspected hovered on the tip of her tongue. Instead, she murmured, "Where's the bathroom?"

He directed her, then excused himself long enough to freshen up, as well. He returned to find her fully tucked and buttoned and preparing to leave. "There's something I want to ask you," he told her. "Actually, it's the reason I invited you to lunch."

A smile flirted with her mouth, a genuine one that filled him with fierce pleasure. "You mean, you didn't invite me so we could indulge in a wrestling match on your couch?"

He regarded her with a hint of laughter. "As delightful as that was, no." He crossed to her side. Unable to resist, he slipped a hand into her hair. Cupping the back of her head, he took her mouth in a swift, hungry kiss, a kiss she returned without hesitation. "Come work for me," he offered when they broke apart.

Her eyes were alight with a slumberous passion and he suspected she didn't assimilate his offer immediately. He saw the instant words connected with comprehension. The passion eked away, replaced by astonishment. "Work for you?" she repeated.

"I can offer you a far better salary than you receive at Timeless, excellent benefits, your own studio. You'll have the Dante name behind your designs." He pressed, determined she see how much more he could do for her than the Fontaines. "I can assist you become one of the most sought-after designers in the world. Best of all, we won't have to sneak around hiding our relationship from your employers."

She took a hasty step away from him, pulling free of his hold, if not the connection burning between them. It refused to release either one of them. "Let me get this straight.

You're offering me a job so we can continue our affair?"

"Of course not." Honesty compelled him to admit, "Okay, fine. In part. But mostly because you're a damn good designer. Dantes would be lucky to have you."

Her eyes narrowed. "And what happens when we're no longer Infernoed?"

The word provoked a swift smile. "Infernoed?"

"Right now, the hot, southern climes of your anatomy are doing your thinking. Once that brilliant mind of yours kicks in, you'll regret any decisions you make while in the throes of this thing. And I'll have thrown away a job I love for a position at Dantes as the ex-mistress of the owner. How long do you think that'll work?"

He struggled not to take offense. Until two nights ago his southern climes had never before overruled the cooler, dispassionate northern half of his body. Yet, he suspected Francesca assumed it happened on a regular basis. It was part of the price he paid for having a Latin name. Emotion over intellect. Total nonsense, of course.

"I won't compromise the family business for anyone or anything," he stated. "My offer is genuine, Inferno or no Inferno. When our affair ends, you'll still have your job, and it'll be a hell of a lot more secure than your future at Timeless."

He could tell she didn't believe him. "Thank you, but I'm happy with the Fontaines."

"Would you at least allow me to make an official offer?"

She dismissed the idea with a swift shake of her head. "I have my reasons for staying at Timeless Heirlooms, and money isn't really one of them. I'm up for a permanent position there. In fact, I would have it already if I hadn't ruined my reputation by spending the night with you. The only saving grace is they don't know it's you."

He thought fast. "We can be discreet. They don't have to know."

She cut him off with a swift shake of her head. "Forget it. I won't make that sort of foolish mistake again or do anything to jeopardize my standing with the Fontaines. And just so we're clear? Being with you could get me fired and my job's more important than anything else." She spared a swift glance toward the couch where the cushions still showed the imprint of their entwined bodies. Still held the heat of their passion. "Even that."

"Francesca—"

She waved him silent. "Forget it, Sev. I agreed to meet with you this one last time.

I think you'll agree it was a lovely way to conclude our affair. And that's all this is. A brief affair, now concluded. Now, I really need to go." She picked up her purse and slung it over her shoulder. "If I don't come back from lunch in a reasonable length of time, they'll start asking questions I can't answer."

It would be pointless to argue, he could tell. Better to find out what Nicolò and Lazz had dug up regarding the gorgeous Ms. Sommers. That way he'd be in a stronger position to formulate a new plan, one with a better chance of success. And it had to be quick, before his North surrendered to his South.

"I'll arrange for a cab," he limited himself to saying. "And I'll give you a call later this week."

She gave him a remote smile. "There's no need . . . on either count."

He watched the delicious sway of her hips as she exited the room, the view threatening to bring him to his knees. "Damn, woman," he muttered. "There's every need. And I plan to prove it to you."

But he'd better figure out how, and fast. Because if he'd learned nothing else as a result of the past few hours, he'd discovered how wrong he'd been about The Inferno and all matters related to it.

He'd been determined to woo Francesca away from the Fontaines and have her work for Dantes. To tempt her—not with sex—but with the financial advantages of working for Dantes. Or that had been his intention until he'd come face-to-face with one incontrovertible fact. A fact that sent his carefully laid plans crumbling to dust. There was no way in hell he could keep his hands off her now, or anytime in the near future. As of this minute, the plan changed.

Not only did he want to uproot her from Timeless Heirlooms so the company would be more vulnerable to a Dantes' takeover, but he also wanted to transplant Francesca into his bed and keep her there.

At least until The Inferno burned itself out.

Chapter Five

Foolishly, Francesca assumed she'd seen the last of Sev.

The delusion lasted right up until she decided to eat lunch at her desk, ordering from her favorite deli, a place that offered fast delivery service and thick sandwiches, stuffed with every imaginable delicacy. Within thirty minutes her sandwich arrived, along with a sprig of vivid-blue forget-me-nots, their delicate scent sweetening the air in her tiny office.

"Thank you," she said to the delivery boy before burying her nose in the fragrant blossoms. "What a nice thing to do."

He eyed her speculatively. "Do I get an extra tip for bein' so nice?"

"Absolutely." She handed it over with a smile. "And thanks again."

"No sweat. The flowers weren't from me, by the way. There's a note that came with them. I stuck it in the bag with your sandwich." With a cheeky grin he darted from the office.

She couldn't help but laugh at his audacity. Then curiosity got the better of her. She opened the bag and found a business card tucked inside. She glanced at it and, to her dismay, her fingers trembled. Sure enough, the linen-colored pasteboard had Sev's name and business information typed on the front. On the back, he'd scrawled *Remember*.

Somehow, he'd figured out where she usually ordered lunch. And for some reason, she spent the rest of the day sniffing the forget-me-nots as she struggled to do as he asked and remember . . . remember that dating Sev promised a fast end to a short career. Worse, it would put an even faster end to her burgeoning relationship with her father. Her mouth firmed. She wouldn't allow anyone—not even a man as sexy as Severo Dante—to interfere with either of those two goals.

The next morning on her way to work, she swung into her favorite Starbucks, desperate for caffeine after a sleepless night of wishing she were in Sev's bed once more. To her dismay, the line stretched long and wide and she schooled herself to patience. Far ahead, toward the front, she caught a glimpse of a distinctive set of shoulders and striking ebony hair. Unbidden, her heart kicked up a notch and the air escaped her lungs in a soft rush.

It wasn't Severo Dante, she silently scolded, and constantly obsessing over him wasn't going to help matters. She refused to see Sev in every man with an impressive build and dark coloring. She needed to get a grip. Deliberately, she forced her gaze away only to catch herself peeking at him as he finished paying and turned to leave.

This time the breath exploded from her in an audible gasp as she realized it *was* Sev. He came directly toward her with the languid grace so uniquely his, carrying a pair of cappuccinos. He handed her one with a warm smile and a quiet, *"Tesoro mio,"* before continuing out the door.

"Oh, God," the woman behind her said with a groan. "Does that happen to you often?"

"No." Francesca stared at the cappuccino, then at the door through which Sev had vanished, before glancing at the woman behind her. "At least . . . not until recently."

"I don't suppose you know what *tesoro mio* means?" Before Francesca could respond, the woman shouted out, "Hey, who knows what *tesoro mio* means?"

"Italian. It means my treasure," an older woman toward the front of the line called back.

"Wow," Francesca's companion in line murmured. "Just, wow."

"I couldn't have said it better myself."

Francesca knocked back the drink Sev had given her in the vain hope it would pull her out of the sensual stupor fogging her brain. It didn't. Instead, she spent the next twenty-four hours daydreaming about him.

The next morning, Friday, she wasted her entire time in line searching in vain for Sev's distinctive build. She refused to be disappointed when she didn't spot him, and even came up with a handful of reasonable excuses for lingering in the small bistro while she sipped her drink. But he never showed.

When she arrived at work, she was stunned to discover a blown-glass vase sitting on her desk with a new flower to replace the forget-me-nots, this time a sprig of orange blossoms. The white star-shaped blooms caressed the flame-red glass, the contrast between the two colors quite striking. Unable to resist, she picked up the vase, the sweet perfume of the flowers flooding her senses while the delicate glasswork warmed within her hold.

It was an incredible piece with sinuous curves that flowed from base to stem and seemed to beg for her touch. Had Sev stroked it, just as she was now doing? Were her fingers tracing the same path his had taken? It was a distinct possibility, since no one who held this gorgeous creation could resist running their fingers along the flowing lines of the fiery glass.

"Oh. *My.*" Tina came to peer over Francesca's shoulder. "I've never seen anything so beautiful. Where did you get it?"

"It's a gift."

"And orange blossoms. *Très romantique!*"

"Really? I didn't know. I just love the scent."

"Mmm. They mean eternal love." Tina's eyes filled with laughter. "Or innocence. I'll let you decide which is more appropriate."

Definitely not innocence. Francesca hastily returned the vase to her desktop. She took a seat and pulled out her sketchpad, determined to get straight to work. Not that she accomplished much. More times than she could count she found herself staring into space with a reminiscent smile on her face while she stroked the vase and inhaled the sweet scent of orange blossoms.

Saturday came and Francesca assumed she wouldn't have to worry about Sev showing up at Starbucks, or sending her a gift at work, or finding some other way to tempt her into giving in to his blatant seduction. Or so she thought until she opened the door to her apartment to his latest surprise.

"What are you doing here?" she demanded.

Sev lowered the fist he'd been about to use on her door. "I came to talk to you."

"I thought we decided we weren't going to contact each other again," she said. "Nothing can come of this, you realize that, don't you? No matter how much I might want to see you, it means losing my job, and I won't risk that."

He stared down at her with such heat that it was a wonder it didn't turn the air to steam. "I'm well aware of that fact. Not that it changes anything." He glanced over her shoulder and into her apartment. "Aren't you going to invite me in?"

"No, I'm not."

"Please, Francesca."

Just those two words and she felt her resolve fading. "What's the point, Sev?" she whispered.

"This. This is the point."

He cupped her face and took her mouth in a passionate kiss. Francesca closed her eyes as Sev made his point, as well as several others, in ways sweeter and more generous than any that had gone before. She gave herself up to sheer rapture, surrendering to desire over common sense. Without even realizing it, she backed into her apartment and Sev kicked the door closed behind them. Endless minutes passed before she surfaced with a groan.

"I can't believe we're doing this again. It's not safe." She fisted her hands in his shirt.

"Listen to me, Sev. I'm telling you straight out. You can't show up at Starbucks or send me flowers or any more gorgeous vases—thank you, by the way—or slip me notes in my lunch."

"Fine. I won't. Instead, why don't I steal you away for the weekend?"

She had to give him credit for sheer brazenness, if nothing else. "Forget it. I've already told you—"

He nodded impatiently. "Yeah, yeah. Heard it all before. That still doesn't change anything. We need time together in order to resolve our differences."

"We can't resolve our differences," she emphasized. "There are simply too many obstacles."

"Obstacles we haven't made any effort to overcome. I'd like to try and correct that oversight. I've made reservations. We'll be discreet. No one will find out we've been together."

"And if I say no?" she asked, lifting an eyebrow. "Will you blackmail me again?"

"Would that make it easier for you to surrender?" His voice dropped, reminding her of a certain moonlit night when he'd whispered the most outrageous suggestions in her ear, suggestions he'd then turned from proposition to action. "Come with me, Francesca. Or I swear

I'll show up at Timeless and tell everyone who'll listen that we're lovers."

"I don't believe you. You're just saying that because—"

He leaned in, stopping her with another endless kiss. "Don't challenge me." There was no mistaking the warning in his dark eyes. "When have I ever failed to follow through on my word?"

"Right now," she informed him. "All this week. You said—" She hesitated, struggling to recall precisely what he had said when they last met. As far as she could remember, she'd done most of the talking that day. He gave her a knowing look and she blew out her breath in an aggravated sigh. "Okay, fine. You might not have come right out and said it, but you did agree to end the affair."

He tipped her face up to his. "Does it look like I agree with our ending things?"

Not even a little. "Without question."

His slow, knowing smile proved her undoing. "Go pack a bag. We can finish arguing about it in the car."

She turned without another word and crossed to her bedroom. Five minutes later she returned with an overnight bag, more certain with every step she took that she'd completely lost her mind. And maybe she had, but after five minutes with Sev, she no longer cared. One more weekend and then she'd put an end to their relationship, she promised herself. Just these two days together and then no more. After all, who would it hurt?

To her delight, Sev drove them into wine country, where he'd booked a room at a charming bed-and-breakfast. They spent the day at several of the local wineries sampling the wares before enjoying an impromptu picnic that consisted of generous slices of the local Sonoma Jack cheese and freshly baked bread. That night they dined out at a small, elegant restaurant specializing in French cuisine, their day together one of the most enchanting Francesca had ever experienced. The sun had long since set when they returned to their room and silently came together.

She'd been waiting for this from the moment she'd agreed to spend the weekend with Sev, had been anticipating it, desire fomenting with each passing hour. And now that the moment had arrived, she tumbled, falling headlong into his arms and into his bed, if not into his heart. Because she couldn't quite convince herself that what they felt could be anything more than physical.

"We can make this work," he told her, during the still hours between deepest night and earliest morning. "If we agree not to discuss anything job-related, this will work."

"For how long?" she protested.

"Look, I know TH is after a big-name actress to pull them out of their financial hole. Eventually, I'll find out who she is. I don't need you for that. There are far more interesting ways to spend my time with you."

She managed a smile, even though she continued to worry. "Our jobs mean everything to us, Sev. Even you can't deny that. They're as much a part of us as our flesh and bones. We won't be able to share that part of ourselves."

He conceded the point with a swift nod. "We'll discuss other things, instead."

"Like what?"

He rolled onto his side to face her. "Like, growing up in foster care. Coming from such a huge family, I can't begin to imagine it. Why were you never adopted?"

She tugged the sheet over her breasts and tucked it beneath her arms. A ridiculous reaction, she conceded, and more than a little telling. But talking about her childhood left her exposed. Any covering, even a sheet, helped compensate for that.

"I almost was," she said in answer to his question. "When I was eight. I'd been in foster care for three years by then."

He traced a scorching finger from the curve of her cheek down the length of her neck. As always, she flamed beneath his touch, her breath growing ragged. "What happened?"

Francesca shrugged. "They were about to adopt me when Carrie unexpectedly became pregnant with twins. The doctor ordered complete bed rest and her husband insisted I be placed elsewhere because it was too much for his wife. I heard him tell the social worker that taking care of me put their babies at risk, and that the babies were their most important consideration."

Sev swept her hair back from her face, regarding her with heartbreaking compassion. "What happened then?"

"I went through a succession of homes after that. Four, I think." She dismissed the memory with a careless smile and rolled over on top of him. His warmth became her warmth and helped diminish the coldness that streaked through her veins and sank into her bones. A coldness those particular memories always engendered. "Acting out, I guess, because I'd been foolish enough to imagine that Carrie and her husband might actually want me as much as the children they were about to have."

"I'm sorry." He released his breath in a rough sigh, causing the curls at her temples to swirl and dance. "That's such an inadequate thing to say. But I mean it."

"Like I said, don't feel sorry for me." Pity was the last thing she wanted from him. "I survived."

"And found your father. That must have helped." He studied her curiously. "You haven't told me anything about him. What's he like?"

"There's not much to tell," she claimed, aware of how evasive she sounded. "He . . . he had a one-night stand with my mother. Since he was married at the time—is still married—I didn't feel comfortable intruding in their lives."

Sev swore. "You just can't catch a break, can you?"

"What about you?" She deliberately changed the subject. "You've said that after your father's death you had to dismantle most of Dantes. I gather that included Timeless Heirlooms."

"Yes."

She could tell he didn't want to talk about it, but pushed, anyway. "Which explains why you're so determined to get it back again. That must have been as difficult for you as foster care was for me." She hesitated before asking, "Why has it become such an obsession? I mean, if your

father was the one responsible for Dantes'
decline—"

He wrapped his arms around her and
reversed their positions, bracing himself on his
forearms to lessen the press of weight on top of
her. "Why have I become so obsessed with
rebuilding it?"

He looked so fierce. So determined. "Yes."

"Because my father tried to tell me
something about the business the day before he
died." His words grew ragged. "And I was too
impatient to listen to another of his crazy
schemes. Maybe if I had—" He broke off,
a muscle jerking in his cheek.

"What?" Her eyes widened in sudden
comprehension. "You think he had an idea for
saving Dantes? One that didn't involve
dismantling the entire business?"

"I don't think. I know. He called it Dante's
Heart. Even my mother thought it would work.
I—*reluctantly*—agreed to meet with them the
next day when they returned from their sailing
excursion."

"Only they didn't return."

He closed his eyes, grief carving deep lines
into his face. "No."

"Didn't he write down his idea? Leave some
sort of clue behind?"

"I tore both home and office apart looking for it. There was nothing. Nothing except—"

She recalled what he'd told her when they'd visited his Pacific Heights house. "Letters detailing his affair with a designer."

"Yes." His mouth slid into a smile. Without fail, that simple quirk of his lips caused her body to quicken in anticipation. "Seems to run in the family."

She acknowledged his comment with a sad smile before returning to the heart of the matter. "You think if you'd only taken the time to listen to your father, you wouldn't have had to sell off all the Dante subsidiaries?"

His hands swept over her, settling on the softest of her curves. "If you're asking whether I blame myself, I'll make it easy for you. I do."

She fought to speak through her shiver of desire. "Seems we both have something to prove."

"So it does." He traced a path of kisses from the hollow of her throat downward. "The first thing I want to prove is how much I want you."

In the hours that followed he did precisely that. Their lovemaking took on a desperate edge, as though beneath the passion they sensed how much they needed one another.

Sev gave no quarter. He took with a ruthless power Francesca couldn't resist. He branded her with his fire, taking her to heights she'd never, ever experienced before, taking her in ways she'd never, ever experienced before. The level of intimacy should have terrified her, the knowledge he gained over her body, and even more overwhelming, her heart, allowing her nowhere to hide.

He forced her from hiding and into the light, forced her to connect with him on every possible level. She might have resisted, but for one thing. He gave every bit as much of himself as he took, baring himself to her need, her touch. Her desire. And in doing so, filling the emptiness within.

Their weekend together changed everything, convincing Francesca that maybe she could have it all. Despite the small warning voice, she couldn't quite silence, she allowed herself to be talked back into Sev's bed. Or blackmailed there, he frequently claimed with a teasing grin.

As the days slid into weeks, she became more and more certain Sev didn't have an ulterior motive, other than to get her in his bed as often as possible. But since that was her motivation, as well, nothing could make her happier. Of course, he continued to offer her a job at Dantes at regular intervals, making the tempting offers as such casual asides they felt more like a joke than a true offer. Foolishly, she even managed to convince herself he'd forgotten about identifying which actress Timeless Heirlooms hoped to sign as their spokeswoman.

Or so she believed until he picked her up one evening and handed her a brightly wrapped package. "This is for you. Fair warning, I want major good-guy points for this one."

"That depends." She picked up the box and shook it. "What did you get?"

"Something you mentioned last week. Go on and open it. It's just a DVD." His expression turned gloomy. "It has chick flick written all over it, but for you, I'm willing to take it like a man."

Ripping off the outer wrapping she realized he'd bought her the latest Juliet Bloom release. She stiffened, wondering if this was his subtle way of telling her he knew about the possibility of TH using Bloom as their spokeswoman. "Thanks," she murmured. She cleared her throat, forcing a more natural tone to her voice. "I can't wait to watch this."

"Then we'll do it tonight," he responded promptly. "We'll order in Chinese and crack open that bottle of Pinot Grigio my family sent over from Italy."

All through the beginning of the movie she remained on edge, praying she wouldn't do or say something to give away TH's plans. The entire time, Sev remained his normal self. As far as she could tell, he didn't watch her with any more intensity than usual. There were no double entendres or suspicious comments. Halfway through the film, she managed to relax and even enjoy herself, perhaps in part due to the glass of wine Sev kept topped off.

By the end of the movie, she was in her usual position whenever they watched a DVD, on the couch curled up in Sev's arms. Tears filled her eyes as the film reached its stunning climax, a scene in which the heroine stood before the villain, clothed in nothing but defiance and diamonds.

"It reminds me of our first night together," Sev murmured. "You were wearing your amethyst-and-diamond set, remember? Bloom would look stunning in one of your designs."

Francesca couldn't tear her eyes from the film. "Yes, she will," she murmured.

It took a full half-dozen heartbeats before she realized what she'd said. It took even less time to realize he'd understood the implications. She ripped free of his embrace and stood. "Oh, God."

Sev climbed slowly to his feet, holding up his hands in a placating gesture. "Honey, don't. Don't overreact. I swear to you, I already knew."

She shook her head, not believing him. "This was a setup, wasn't it?"

"Not even a little."

Tears of anger blurred her vision. "And I fell for it. I got complacent. Even when I saw which movie you'd chosen, I convinced myself not to read anything into it." The breath hitched in her throat as she looked around for her purse. "I have to go."

"No, you don't," he argued. "You need to stay so we can talk this through."

She ignored him, scooping her purse off the coffee table and crossing to the entryway to snatch her sweater from the antique armoire he used as a coat closet. "Just answer me one question, Sev." She spun to face him. "Are you going to use the information about Juliet Bloom to try and take down TH?"

At least he didn't lie to her. "Yes."

"Then there's nothing left to be said, is there?"

"There's more to be said than you can possibly imagine. But since you're in no mood to listen to me tonight, it can wait until tomorrow."

"You're wrong, Sev." She yanked open the door to his apartment and stepped through. "There is no tomorrow for us."

Chapter Six

The answer to Francesca's question—was Sev going to use the information she'd let slip?—came the next morning when she rushed in to work.

A message sat on her desk requesting she report to Tina's office at her earliest convenience. It didn't have anything to do with her slipup, she attempted to convince herself. Not this fast, nor this soon. He'd only had one night to track down the actress or her rep and cause trouble. He couldn't possibly have accomplished that so quickly.

But a feeling of impending doom clung to her as she sprinted up the steps to the executive level of Timeless Heirlooms. The Fontaines shared adjoining offices at one end of the floor and she could hear Tina's voice raised in anger coming from her side of the suite. Not unusual, given her volatile nature. But not welcome, either, all things considered. Kurt's placating voice rumbled in response to whatever Tina said, indicating the two were in there together.

Francesca knocked on the door, not in the least surprised when no one answered. She doubted they heard her over the shouting. Peeking around the door, she asked, "You wanted to see me?"

Kurt waved her in and toward a brilliant magenta sofa at one end of the room. She took a seat and waited. Outside, storm clouds marched across the city skyline, a perfect reflection of the Fontaines' mood.

"I'm serious, Kurt. Something has to be done about them."

"What do you suggest, honey?" He shoved a hand through hair a shade paler than Francesca's own honey-blond. "I've called Juliet Bloom's rep every day since the showing. She's polite, but refuses to commit."

"Because of those damn Dantes!"

Francesca stiffened at hearing her worst fears confirmed. "What have the Dantes got to do with Juliet Bloom?" As if she didn't know.

Tina swung around, only too happy to explain. "Surprise, surprise, they've approached her, too." She slammed her hands down on her desk. "They sell wedding rings, for God's sake, not jewelry sets. But because it's the Dante name, Bloom is listening."

Francesca's heart sank. Oh, God. He'd done it. Somehow, he'd used her slip of the tongue to wrestle the Bloom account away from the Fontaines. "When . . . when did this happen?"

"We're not sure. Bloom's been cagey ever since the show. Promising, but never quite committing. Then this morning we found out why."

Francesca closed her eyes to hide the guilt she knew must be readily apparent. This was all her fault. She should have been up front with the Fontaines from the start. She never should have allowed Sev to convince her to continue their affair, despite the hint of blackmail behind his insistence. But she'd wanted him, wanted him desperately. And so she'd caved when she should have held firm. If TH went under, she'd be the one responsible and they'd never forgive her. Hell, she'd never forgive herself.

"What are you going to do?" she finally asked.

Tina resumed her pacing. "What can we do? We're running out of time." She didn't need to add that a good portion of Timeless Heirlooms' future hung on the actress agreeing to be their spokeswoman and wear Francesca's creations in her next picture.

Kurt glanced at Francesca. "Severo Dante called," he murmured in an aside. "He told us he was behind the delay and upped his offer for Timeless."

Day Leclaire

Tina glared in frustration. "I don't care what that SOB offers. I'm not selling." Her anger crumbled to panic and she barreled straight into Kurt's arms. "We're in this together, right? United we stand and all that? Because I couldn't do this without you. This place would fall apart if it weren't for you."

His arms tightened around his wife. "I'm not going anywhere. We'll figure something out."

Tears stung Francesca's eyes at the open display of affection. If only she'd had that sort of unconditional love and protection growing up. She shook her head, refusing to allow her thoughts to go there. It wouldn't serve any purpose other than to drive her crazy with futile longing. Kurt could never be her father. And Sev would never be anything more than her temporary lover.

After all, it didn't matter that she couldn't claim Kurt as her father, she decided then and there, or reveal her connection to him. She refused to do anything that might damage the Fontaines' marriage. And finding out that Kurt had not only indulged in an affair in the early years of their marriage, but also that a child had resulted from the affair, would do more than damage it. Knowing Tina, it could very well destroy thirty years of wedded bliss. Francesca could barely handle the guilt of her part in bringing down TH. It would destroy her if she

123 | P a g e

ruined Kurt and Tina's marriage, on top of everything else.

Just being this close to her father filled Francesca with more joy than she thought possible. After all the lonely years in foster care, all the years of working every spare minute of every day to hone her craft, she'd settle for whatever scraps she could get. She refused to bemoan her current circumstances. While her connection to family would remain tenuous at best, as long as she worked at Timeless Heirlooms and it remained afloat, she could pursue a career she loved with all her heart and soul. Even better, she could remain in her father's orbit, even if she never became one of his inner circle.

And if that meant helping them beat Sev at his own game, so be it. "Is there anything I can do?" she asked. "Is there some way of convincing Juliet Bloom to go with TH?"

Kurt looked at her over Tina's head. "Put out some feelers among your associates. See if you can find out who this new designer is."

She froze. "I'm sorry. What new designer?"

Tina pulled free of Kurt's embrace. "That's right. We didn't tell her the best part. Wait until you hear." She planted her hands on her hips. "Dantes has convinced Bloom's people that they have some hot new designer on the hook who can give Dame Juliet exactly what she wants."

Oh, no. Oh, please don't let it be who she thought it was. "Who? Who's their new designer?"

"We have no idea. We haven't heard so much as a whisper of a rumor."

"That's where you come in," Kurt added. "We'd appreciate it if you'd keep your ear to the ground. See what some of the other designers are saying. It has to be someone they've acquired very recently, since this Bloom deal's only been around for the past few weeks."

"Maybe we should go downstairs and count heads," Tina muttered. "See if any of our designers are missing. It would be just like him to snitch one of them right from under our noses."

Francesca closed her eyes, her world tilting. Aware that the Fontaines waited for her response, she swallowed, struggling to speak around a throat gone bone-dry. "I'll see what I can find out."

Not that it would take much effort. In fact, it wouldn't take much more than a single visit. How many times had Sev offered her a job, each proposition more lucrative than the last? Suddenly, it all made sense.

Sev knew that TH was in hot negotiation with some big name. He'd been frank about that almost from the start. Chances were excellent he also knew which designer had piqued that person's interest, had undoubtedly known from the night they first met.

If he stole—*seduced*—her away from TH, he'd gain the ultimate prize. Now that he'd romanced the actress's name out of her, he'd land a highly lucrative account with Bloom *and* take away the Fontaines' best chance at revitalizing the company Dantes wanted to purchase. If she didn't miss her guess, Sev planned to use her to accomplish both those goals.

Overhead the storm clouds broke.

Francesca didn't give the assistant seated at a desk outside Sev's door a chance to stop her. She simply swept past the stunning blonde and barged straight into his office. Four men sat sprawled on couches and chairs in an informal sitting area at the far end of the enormous room. She recognized them from the photos that decorated the console in Sev's den, as well as the walls of his apartment.

The Dantes, all four glorious male specimens on display.

Sharp light, scrubbed clean from the recent storm, streamed from the floor-to-ceiling windows and haloed the twins, Marco and Lazz, who sat opposite each other like a pair of striking bookends. She pegged Marco by his wide grin and appreciative gaze, not to mention the sexual sizzle he gave off with every exhalation. Lazz regarded her with a cool, analytical stare, everything about him suggesting a man who kept his emotions under tight control. And then there was Nicolò, the youngest at twenty-nine, but according to Sev, the most dangerous of the bunch. Had he been the one to suggest her as a creative solution for taking over Timeless Heirlooms? Finally, her attention switched to Sev.

He knew why she'd come. She saw the knowledge settle across a face she'd covered with sweet kisses just a few hours earlier. He jerked his head toward the door and his brothers stood en masse. Before Nicolò left, he handed Sev a file folder with her name prominently displayed across the cover.

Sev lobbed the opening volley. "I have one question before you say anything. Have you signed a formal contract yet with Timeless Heirlooms, or are you still on probation?"

She couldn't believe his nerve. "That's none of your business," she retorted, stung.

"Answer me, Francesca." His quiet tone gentled the implacable demand. "Have you signed with them?"

"I intend to, just as soon as I tell you what I think of you."

He simply nodded, but she caught a hint of relief that came and went in his expression. "Would you care to sit?"

"I prefer to do this standing." Her hands curled into fists. "You used me. You used me to try and take over TH. I'm here to tell you that you've failed. And I'm also here to tell you that I think you're despicable."

"Let's set the record straight on several points." He stood, tossing the folder Nicolò had given him to one side. "When we first met—*hell,* when we first made love—I had no idea who you were. Maybe if I'd answered my cell when Marco phoned that night, I would have. But if you recall, I was a little preoccupied and he didn't get through to me until the next morning."

She folded her arms across her chest and shook her head. "I'm not buying it. You could have discovered my identity before you ever arrived at the showing."

"It would have been possible, I suppose. But the fact is, I didn't." He stalked closer. "Next point. The Fontaines and I were already negotiating the sale of Timeless Heirlooms before you and I ever met. Tina knew I intended to buy them out, either when she eventually sold out to me, or after she was forced to declare bankruptcy. That hasn't changed."

"But you hadn't counted on the success of the showing."

"No."

"Or that they might acquire Juliet Bloom as their spokeswoman. Or that she would use their collection in her next film."

"Correction. *Your* collection. And Juliet Bloom has postponed her decision." He paused a beat. "Indefinitely."

Undisguised fury ripped through Francesca. "Because you told her you had a collection as good as TH's, along with the perfect designer. Me." He didn't deny it and desolation battled with anger. "You thought you could hire me away from the Fontaines and steal the Bloom account so they'd be forced to sell to you."

"Yes."

The simple confirmation cut deep. "You're not even going to deny it?" *Please deny it!*

"Why should I? It's true. If you'd accepted my job offer that's exactly how it would have gone down." For the first time, she saw a businessman instead of her lover. "That's how it's still going down."

She shook her head, so angry she could barely see straight. So heartbroken she could barely feel past the pain. "Not a chance in hell.

Do you think I'd ever agree to work for you after this? That I'll ever sleep with you again?"

"One has nothing to do with the other. One is business, the other personal." He shrugged. "The two are mutually exclusive."

Her chin wobbled precariously. Didn't he get it? "One has everything to do with the other. I've lived a lifetime of betrayal in one form or another. I can't . . ." She ground to a halt, correcting herself. "I *won't* be with a man I can't trust."

"Francesca, I didn't seduce you in order to tempt you away from Timeless."

Liar! "You actually expect me to believe that?"

"It's the truth. I made you a legitimate job offer for two reasons. First, you'd be an incredible asset to Dantes. You're the best designer I've ever seen, and that's saying a lot."

"And second?" Not that she needed him to spell it out. She already knew.

"Second, having you leave TH makes them more vulnerable to a Dantes' takeover."

Did he really think she'd find his reasoning appropriate? That A plus B equaled acceptable in her book? He had a lot to learn. "Maybe if you only wanted me because of my talent, I could somehow justify it. Somehow. But that's not the case. You want to take down Timeless Heirlooms and you want to use me to do it. I can't allow that. I can't allow you to do anything that threatens Tina and Kurt."

"Because Kurt's your father."

The breath escaped her lungs in a heady rush and her vision blurred. One minute she stood staring at Sev in utter betrayal and the next he pressed her into one of the nearby chairs. He disappeared from her line of sight for a moment, then returned with glass in hand.

"It's just water, though I have something stronger if you prefer."

She shook her head without speaking and downed the water in a desperate gulp. *"How? How could you possibly know that?"*

"Nicolò hired a private investigator." Sev cupped the curve of her cheek and for a brief, insane moment she relaxed into his touch. The instant she realized what she'd done, she jerked back and his hand fell away. "Before we met at Le Premier I arranged to have each designer investigated. Marco and I attended the showing in order to collect names. By the time Nicolò called the next morning, the PI had matters well underway."

"You're going to blackmail me now, aren't you?"

"Yes."

She closed her eyes. Oh, God. He made it seem so simple. So obvious and acceptable. "You're a total bastard, you know that?"

"When it comes to taking care of my family, you're right." She could literally feel the change come over him as he shifted from lover to adversary. "I'd rather you come to us of your own free will. But I'll do whatever necessary to restore Dantes."

She looked at him, searching his face for some sign of the man she'd taken to her bed. If he still existed—if he *ever* existed—he was lost to her now. "Don't do this," she pleaded. "You don't need TH. Dantes will still be a success without hurting Tina and Kurt."

"Their business is failing." She hated the compassion gleaming in his burnished gold eyes. Hated him all the more for being right. "Bloom might revitalize it for a short time, but Tina is too capricious to keep the business going for longer than a few years. She hired three designers, two of whom are worse than mediocre. The fact that she also hired you is more dumb luck than true discernment. The only reason the company hasn't gone under before this is thanks to Kurt's business acumen."

"So now you're the hero? You're going to rescue Timeless Heirlooms?"

He gathered himself, exuding an uncompromising determination that had long been a hallmark of the Dante legend. "Timeless Heirlooms belonged to us. Because of my father's own capriciousness, I had no choice but to sell it off. Now I'm in a position to right that wrong. Do you expect me to walk away without recovering what I lost?" Regret colored his words. "That isn't going to happen and you know it."

"Because you feel responsible for Dantes' fall from grace?"

"Because I *am* responsible. You know why I feel that way."

She remembered the night he'd explained it to her, and how sympathetic she'd felt. Not anymore. Not when he demonstrated such ruthless disregard in order to achieve his goal. "So, you'll do anything to return the company to its former glory. No matter who gets hurt. No matter who gets in your way or who you have to steamroll over." She wasn't asking, but acknowledging fact.

"No one has to get hurt. The Fontaines will be in a far better position if they sell out to us now than if I'm forced to collect the broken pieces after their fall."

"Very generous of you, I'm sure."

For the first time, a spark of anger flared to life in his eyes. "It's time to negotiate, Francesca.

Will you come to work at Dantes of your own volition?"

"What happens if I refuse? Will you tell Tina that I'm Kurt's daughter?"

For the first time he didn't give her a straight answer. "I don't want to do it that way."

"But you will if you think there's no other option. You will because you know that the news will devastate Tina, since she and Kurt were married at the time of my conception. Knowing how volatile she is, she'll throw him out. And even if they eventually reconcile—which they will since they truly love each other—the damage will have been done. Their neglect will hand you TH."

"That's Nicolò's assessment of the situation, yes."

"It's a rotten thing to do, Sev."

Pain sliced across his face. "I've been forced to make far more difficult decisions, decisions that have had a disastrous impact on people's lives." His voice dropped, landed in some dark, desolate place that echoed through his words. "I've had no choice. No one else could make those decisions. And I don't doubt there'll be other occasions when I'm forced to make more."

She could see the truth in his eyes, see that he'd made an uncomfortable home for himself between that proverbial rock and a hard place.

She could also sympathize with him, up to a point. Because from now on she'd have to make difficult decisions as well, to stand on her own without Sev at her back. Well, she'd been there before, just as Sev had. She'd lived most of her life with no one beside her when times grew tough. She could do it again. She needed to be strong, to refortify the barriers she'd created years ago to hide her vulnerability and weakness. And she would. There wasn't any other choice.

"If I agree to work with you, I have one request." She didn't allow herself to consider that her statement as good as conceded defeat.

"Name it."

"The Fontaines are to receive full price for TH. I want it in my contract. I won't lift a finger to help Dantes otherwise."

He gave it a moment's reflection. "In that case I want an exclusive two-year contract with you with an additional two-year non-compete clause. If you walk away without meeting the terms of your contract, I won't allow you to work for anyone else in the industry in any capacity, whatsoever, for two full years."

Suddenly she found herself right there with him, a hard place boring into her back, a boulder slamming her from the front. "That seems a bit harsh."

"I have an investment to protect. I have no intention of buying out TH only to have you walk away from Dantes and help the Fontaines start up a competing business."

It hadn't occurred to her to do any such thing. But now that he mentioned it, it would serve him right if she'd planned to do precisely that. "Very well. I agree."

He held out his hand. "Welcome to Dantes."

Francesca realized her mistake the instant she put her hand in his. The Inferno reared its ugly head, darting from his hand to hers and setting her blood on fire. It didn't seep into her bones, but burned inward, branding her more deeply and completely than she thought possible.

She saw a similar kick of reaction from Sev, the sensation filling his expression with a predatory hunger. "Oh, and there's one more detail I forgot to mention."

She didn't have to ask. She knew precisely what detail he'd omitted. "Forget it."

"I can't forget, any more than you can." Sev's eyes turned to molten gold. "I still want you in my bed."

Chapter Seven

Sev deliberately kept his distance from Francesca over the next few days while she gave notice at TH and settled into her new home at Dantes, not wanting to throw any more fuel on a situation already on the verge of a messy explosion. He'd done enough by insisting she return to his bed, as well as come to work at Dantes.

Though she'd accepted the latter with dignified anger, when it came to his former demand, she'd told him in no uncertain terms which dark corner of his body to put his suggestion and precisely how to achieve such an impossibility. Though he regretted the means he'd used to force her compliance on the work front, at some point she'd face facts.

Timeless Heirlooms teetered on the edge of destruction, and not even Francesca's brilliant designs would save it. Not in the long run. He'd rather acquire TH while he and his brothers could still turn it around, rather than attempt to pick up pieces shattered beyond repair. Quite simply, the Dantes were in a position to fix problems. The Fontaines weren't. Unfortunately, he doubted he'd ever be able to convince Francesca of that simple fact.

He'd respected her preferences and kept his distance, missing her from both his life and his bed. But now Sev couldn't stand it another minute. Whatever existed between them, whether The Inferno or simple desire, the craving to have her close at hand threatened everything he'd worked the past decade to accomplish.

A nagging compulsion consumed him, as though an emergency signal lit up the connection between them. He couldn't recall ever being this distracted. After the sixth time he stood with the subconscious urge to track her down, he finally gave in and acted on the impulse.

He found her in the studio he'd arranged for her use, a huge, bright room with every possible amenity at her disposal, right down to a plush sitting area and tiny kitchenette. Giving her door a brief knock, he entered. And then he allowed his senses to consume him, the thumb of his left hand moving automatically to ply the palm of his right.

She sat at her desk, a drawing pad flipped open and a charcoal pencil in hand. He couldn't say whether the sketch she applied herself to with such assiduous attention had anything to do with her job. But whatever she worked on, he suspected she'd lost all awareness of time and place.

Sunlight streamed from nearby windows and swirled within her hair, spinning the honey-blond strands to pure gold. It also illuminated the creamy tone of her complexion, making her appear lit from within. Even from this distance, he picked up traces of her unique perfume, the scent light and crisp and uniquely hers.

The pressure that had been building over the past few days eased with his first glimpse of her, forcing him to concede just how tense he'd become without constant contact with her. Every instinct begged him to go to her and carry her off. To take her as far from Dantes and the Fontaines as possible.

"Is there something I can help you with, Mr. Dante?" she asked without looking up.

He lifted an eyebrow. "Mr. Dante?" He leaned against the door, forcing it shut.

"Don't."

Just that one word, but it contained a full measure of pain and disillusionment. She looked at him then, sparing him nothing. He knew he'd hurt her, but refused to consider how badly. Until now. More than anything he wished he could go to her and find a way to ease her despair. But not only wouldn't she welcome it, he suspected she'd tear a strip off his hide if he came anywhere near her.

"Do you have any idea what it's like being here?" she continued. "The untenable position you've put me in?"

He cocked his head to one side. Okay... Maybe more was going on than his forcing her to work for him. Something had exacerbated the situation. "What's wrong?" he demanded.

She threw down her pencil and glared at him. "Why did you give me this office?"

He didn't hesitate. "Because it's the best one available."

"Great. Just great. Would you care to know the first question my coworkers asked me?" She didn't wait for his response. "Not my name. Not general questions about my background. Not where I attended school or who I studied with or where I last worked. They wanted to know who I'd slept with to get this studio."

Sev winced. "Hell."

"Oh, it gets better."

She swept a hand toward the pretty little sitting area tucked beneath the windows. "Guess what's now called the 'casting couch'? Of course, my coworkers treat it like a big joke, but I can see the speculation. They're wondering who I am and why I rate such consideration. As far as they're concerned, I'm brand-new to the industry. An apprentice in their eyes. But somehow, I've leapfrogged over them and they don't like it one little bit. In a single thoughtless move, you've made it impossible for me to associate effectively with the other Dante employees."

Damn. "I didn't realize."

"Fine. You didn't realize. But now that you do, you have to fix it."

He could guess where this was going. "What do you suggest?"

"Transfer me to one of the other Dante locations. New York. London. Paris. The way things are right now, I'd even take Timbuktu. Just send me someplace else where they don't know me. Where . . ." She snatched a shaky breath. "Where I don't have to anticipate seeing you around every corner."

Not see her for months on end? He couldn't do it. The mere suggestion threatened what little sanity he had remaining. "Forget it. Not for at least two years."

"Two years?" He hated the cynical light that pitched her eyes to a black both deep and diamond-hard. "Unless The Inferno burns down to ashes before then, right?"

Sev ignored the question. It hit uncomfortably close to home and he hated the thought that his actions could have so base a motivation. "Other than transfer you, what else can I do? Name it and if it's in my power I'll give it to you."

She laughed, the sound so filled with sorrow that he flinched. "You can give me my old life back. You can let me work for the Fontaines again. Live my life the way I choose. I want to work with—" Her voice broke. "With my father. Even if he didn't know about our relationship, at least I could see him every day. At least he didn't hate me."

Sev froze. "Hate you?"

She stared at him in disbelief. "Are you *really* so blind? Didn't it occur to you what would happen when I refused to sign with Kurt and Tina? What would happen when I turned my back on them after all they've done for me? How they'd react when I jumped to Dantes instead of honoring my promise to sign the contract they were on the verge of offering? I betrayed them, Sev. I betrayed them in the cruelest manner possible and they despise me for what I've done to them."

Dammit to hell. He should have anticipated this. His distraction had cost them both. "I'll talk to them."

"And tell them what?" She thrust back her chair and stood, the movement lacking her usual grace. "Don't you get it? I'll be the proximate cause for the Fontaines losing Timeless Heirlooms. I'm the one they'll blame when you take over. Talking to them isn't going to do a bit of good."

He hadn't considered that aspect of the situation for a very simple, yet vital reason. He'd been so focused on his family's business and restoring all he'd been forced to dismantle, that he hadn't fully explored how his decision would impact Francesca. And he could guess why. He didn't dare look too closely or he'd never be able to make the tough calls. Examining the problem from Francesca's side of the fence would also force him to take a long, hard look at his past choices, something he refused to contemplate.

He'd ruined so many lives when he'd sold off the bits and pieces of Dantes. Until then they'd been a premier business, marketing the most exclusive and magnificent jewelry, worldwide. When his father died, he'd been forced into the top position fresh out of college, with little preparation. And even though Primo had come out of retirement during those first difficult days, his grandfather's heart attack, just three short months after the death of his eldest son and daughter-in-law, had put a swift end to his involvement.

From that point on, Sev shouldered the full burden. He, and he alone, had made the tough choices, choices vital to Dantes' survival. He'd been merciless all those years ago. There'd been no other option. One by one, he'd shut down Dantes' subsidiaries, cutting a swath of destruction throughout the company with ruthless disregard for the lives his decisions destroyed. It had been the only way to save the core business. And now here was one more tough choice to add to the lengthy list he'd accepted as part of his "chain of shame."

"I'm sorry," he said, knowing the sentiment to be both inadequate and unwanted.

She turned her back on him. "Is there anything else I can do for you? I need to return to work."

An idea came to him, an idea so outrageous it might have been one of Nicolò's crazier schemes. He didn't give himself time to consider all the ramifications. To pull this off, he needed to act, and act fast. "Actually, there is something else. It's the reason I came here, as a matter of fact. There's a charity auction this Saturday night. Dantes has donated a few wedding rings to help raise money for the Susan G. Koman Breast Cancer Foundation. I need an escort."

Instantly she shook her head. "No, thank you."

"It isn't a request."

She spun to confront him. "You must be joking." One look at his expression and her mouth tightened. "Dating you is now part of my job description?"

"I don't recall referring to Saturday night as a date. It's a business function. And yes, on occasion you'll be expected to attend them, just as the Fontaines expected you to when you worked for TH."

He could see the frustration eating at her. "Why is my presence so important?"

"Because it aligns you with your new employer in a public setting."

She paled. "Will the Fontaines be there?"

"I assume so." Compassion filled him. "You're going to have to face them sometime," he added gently.

For a brief, heartrending moment, her chin trembled. Then she firmed it and squared her shoulders. "Fine. We might as well get it over with. Where is it, and what time should I arrive?"

"It's at Le Premier again." He sympathized with her slight flinch, understanding that she probably regarded the hotel as the scene of her downfall. Or at the very least, the point where her life took a sharp, painful ninety-degree turn. "I'll pick you up at your apartment at eight."

"Not a chance—"

"Don't." He cut her off without compunction. "You're not going to win, so don't waste your energy fighting me."

Her chin shot up. "It's your way or . . . what? You'll fire me?"

He didn't bother answering. She knew the terms of their contract without him reiterating them. He approached, drawn by a force beyond his ability to control. "Do you really want to turn our relationship into a war when there are so many better ways we could expend our time and energy?"

Passion exploded across her face. Unfortunately, anger drove it rather than desire. "I refuse to fall into your arms after you've forced me into this situation. How could you think I would?"

"Then don't fall." He caught her close and offered a teasing smile. "Trip a little and I'll catch you."

Her anger vied with a naked longing and she splayed her hands across his chest to hold him off. "Please don't do this, Sev. Either let me work for you or let me go. But if you keep forcing the issue, we'll end up despising each other."

He tucked a lock of hair behind her ear, the silken feel of her curls rivaling that of her skin. "I could never despise you." His smile tilted. "But maybe that's all you feel for me."

She closed her eyes. "I—I don't despise you."

He knew how hard her confession came. He leaned into her, basking in her feminine warmth. Somehow, someway, he'd find a way to fix this, while still protecting Dantes and all the people who depended on him.

Somehow.

Francesca dressed with more than her usual care. She tried to tell herself she did it for her own peace of mind, that the extra pains she took helped give her the strength and composure she needed to face the Fontaines, as well as others in the industry who felt she'd sold out. But that would be a lie. Everything she did to prepare for the night ahead was with one person in mind.

Sev.

She checked the mirror a final time. The sleek bronze-toned dress hugged her curves, while her hairstyle, a simple knot at the base of her neck, helped draw attention to the topaz chandelier earrings she'd designed before joining Timeless Heirlooms. In fact, it had been one of the pieces that convinced Kurt and Tina to hire her. Checking the mirror a final time, she nodded in satisfaction. Simple and understated, while subtly advertising why her talents were currently in such high demand. Or at least she hoped that would be the overall reaction.

Promptly at eight, Sev knocked at her door. His single sweeping look convinced Francesca she'd chosen the perfect ensemble. Hot molten hunger exploded in his gaze. She fell back a step before the wall of heat radiating off him. Heaven help her, when had her apartment grown so small? And when had Sev grown so large? Even worse, after everything he'd done, why did she still long to throw herself in his arms and surrender everything to him? It didn't make a bit of sense.

"Tesoro mio," he murmured. The lyricism she'd come to associate with him caressed the words. "You stagger me."

Good. She wanted him staggered. She wanted to knock him clean off his feet. It seemed only fair considering he'd done the same to her. Not that she'd allow any hint of that to show. Behind her, the bed called to her, whispering such innovative suggestions, it brought a blush to her cheeks. She gathered up her wrap and purse. Time to leave. She didn't dare stay another second in such close confines with Sev. Not with her bed misbehaving. Stupid bed.

She suffered the short drive to Le Premier in silence, reluctant to do or say anything that might put her mental and emotional state in jeopardy. The next few hours would prove incredibly difficult and she wanted a few minutes to prepare herself, to slam every barrier she possessed into place. She succeeded beautifully, right up until he helped her from the car.

Leaning down in a sweet, intimate move, he whispered in her ear, "Back to the scene of the crime."

"Yours or mine?" She managed to ask the question with barely a tremor to betray her agitation.

"Mine," he claimed without hesitation. "I accept full blame for what happened here."

"Considering how little resistance I offered, that's rather generous of you."

He gathered her hand in his and tucked it through the crook of his arm. "Not at all. Because if I had to do it over again, I would."

She stiffened in outrage. "You'd blackmail me into leaving the Fontaines?"

He looked down at her, his eyes burning with tarnished lights. "I'd steal you away and make love to you until morning broke." A teasing smile came and went. "And then I'd blackmail you, if only to keep you close."

Francesca didn't know how to respond to his provocative statement, so she remained silent. If he noticed her discomfort, he didn't let on, chatting casually with associates and taking pains to introduce her as "the most talented designer he'd ever met." To her relief, the first part of the evening passed without a hitch. She and Sev wandered through the ballroom, examining the various offerings available for bid. He paused to show her the three pieces Dantes' donated to the cause.

They were all wedding rings, of course. The first she saw featured a "fancy" yellow diamond in a vintage setting that whispered of romantic styles from the late nineteenth century. A Verdonia Royal amethyst complemented the diamond. The second ring appeared more sophisticated, the diamond solitaire a clear stone in a swirl of platinum with a round brilliant cut. But Francesca found it too cold for her taste. Moving on to the third ring, she froze, not even realizing she held her breath until she released it on a prolonged sigh. Never had she seen anything so beautiful.

"Is this a fire diamond?" she asked in amazement.

She'd heard of them, of course, but had never been fortunate enough to see one, let alone use them in any of the jewelry she designed. She'd read that the fire of its transformation from coal to diamond lingered at its very heart and gave the gemstone its name. Sure enough, she could see the flames that licked outward from the fiery depths. Mesmerized, she could only stare in awe.

"There's only one mine that produces them and Dantes owns it," he confirmed. "They're even more rare than pink diamonds."

The fire diamond was breathtaking in its simplicity, and yet the band lifted it from stunning to extraordinary. Woven together into a gorgeous setting that combined gold with white gold, it provided a perfect backdrop for the stone.

"Two disparate halves made one," he explained.

"Oh, Sev," she murmured. "I wish I'd designed this. It's magnificent."

He shot her a look of amusement intermingled with pride. "Primo will be delighted to hear you think so, since he created it. It's one of a kind."

"And you're auctioning it off?" She stared at him in dismay. "How can you bear for it to go out of the family?"

"It's for a good cause."

Over the next few hours Francesca forgot her animosity toward Sev. She had so much fun examining all the donated items, she didn't even remember the Fontaines and the strong possibility she'd run into them. When the time came for Primo's ring to go up on the block, she waited anxiously to see who would claim it. To her surprise, Sev put in the winning bid at the very last minute.

"Now I know why you weren't worried." She gave a wry grin. "I should have known."

He inclined his head. "Yes, you should. Primo would have killed me if I'd lost that final bid. Wait here for a minute while I retrieve it."

He left her side to go and claim the ring. No sooner had he disappeared from sight than she caught a glimpse of the Fontaines. Every other thought fled as she stood frozen in place, utterly vulnerable to the approaching storm. Before they reached her, Sev reappeared with a ring box bearing the distinctive Dantes logo.

Spotting the Fontaines, Sev dropped a hand to her shoulder. "Look at me, sweetheart," he murmured.

"I'm all right. Really. I'm fine." So why did her voice sound so thread and terrified?

"You will be." He gently turned her toward him. Lifting her hand, he slid Primo's ring onto her finger. "Trust me."

She glanced down, stunned. "What are you doing?"

"I'm trying to fix things. To protect you."

"I—I don't understand."

"I need you to go along with what's about to happen." He spoke low and urgently. "I owe you this much, sweetheart. Hell, I owe you far more."

Before she could demand a further explanation, the Fontaines descended. Sev greeted them with a broad smile. "You can be the first to congratulate us." He held up her left hand. The fire diamond caught the light and burst into flames. "Francesca just agreed to marry me."

"You must be kidding." Disbelief overrode Tina's anger. "This is a joke, right?"

Kurt studied Francesca with open concern. "This is sudden."

Did she look as dazed as she felt? Probably. She'd never handled surprises well. She'd learned long ago that surprises meant something unpleasant. Like losing a parent. Like being adopted and then returned. Like moving to a new foster home. "I—"

"She's still in shock," Sev said with an understanding smile. "She didn't see it coming."

"You think I believe this?" Tina demanded. "You think I believe you've actually fallen in love with her?"

Sev tucked Francesca close in a protective hold. "Why do you find it so difficult to believe?" A hard note underscored the question. "Do you consider her so unlovable?"

"Just the opposite," Tina snapped. She started to reach for Francesca before realizing what she'd almost done and snatched her hand back. "It's you I don't trust, Dante. She may be too inexperienced to figure out what you're up to, but I'm not. You've romanced her away from Timeless Heirlooms because she's our best designer. You know perfectly well that without her—" Her voice broke.

It was Kurt's turn to pull his wife into protective arms. "Don't, love. At least now we know what happened."

Tears flooded Francesca's eyes. "I'm sorry," she whispered. "You have no idea how badly I feel."

"Give it time," Tina shot back. "You're going to feel a lot worse before he's done with you. The only reason he's romancing you is to facilitate his takeover of TH. You realize that, don't you?"

Francesca couldn't bring herself to respond to the question. How could she when every word Tina spoke was the truth? Her fingers dug into Sev's arm as she struggled to keep from bursting into tears. She needed to get away. Now. "Excuse me, won't you?"

Spinning free of Sev's embrace, she pushed her way through the crowd of people. She needed air, needed time to regroup. She adored Tina and Kurt, had wanted to spend the bulk of her career working for them. At least, that had been her dream. But Sev changed all that, turning her life upside down.

She gazed down at the engagement ring gracing her finger. And now he'd tried to restore her relationship with the Fontaines. To put himself in the line of fire, instead of her. What he didn't realize was how difficult she found wearing this ring. To her an engagement ring symbolized a soul-deep love. A promise that she'd have someone at her side who cherished her and would be her lifelong partner. This gorgeous, incredible, breathtaking ring was nothing more than a sham. It wasn't real.

And more than ever, it left her feeling like an outsider.

Chapter Eight

Sev stood there, annoyed to discover himself acting the part of the stereotypical hapless male as Francesca disappeared into the crowd in one direction, and an infuriated Tina stormed off in the opposite. Sev stopped Kurt before he could charge after his wife. For Francesca's sake, he had to find a way to make this right.

"Francesca didn't have any choice," Sev stated. "You realize that, don't you?"

Kurt swung around with a snarl, shaking free of Sev's hold. "I realize you forced her to quit a promising job with us and go to work for you."

Sev fought for patience. "It wouldn't have worked, Kurt. It would have put her in an impossible position. Because of our relationship, she'd have been trapped between you and Tina, and the Dantes. She'd have had to watch every word she said, both at work and at home for fear of betraying one side or the other."

Kurt's anger hadn't diminished, but he still stood there, which counted for something. "So, you made her choose between us?"

"Yes. She doesn't deserve your anger. The only thing she's guilty of is falling in love. Her decision hurt you. Trust me when I say that same decision hurt her every bit as much. She adores you and Tina. You've been her mentors. Her friends. Her family. She owes you everything, and don't think she isn't aware of that fact."

Kurt's expression softened ever so slightly, right up until he looked at Sev. "And you?" he asked harshly. "Is Tina right? Is this your clever way of getting your hands on TH?"

"I don't need Francesca to do that. TH will be mine whether she's working for you, or for me."

"Not if I can help it."

"Kurt . . ." Sev grimaced. "Talk to Tina. The two of you are important to Francesca."

"Important enough to get you to back off?"

Sev couldn't prevent a smile. If circumstances had been different he might have formed a friendship with Kurt. He'd prefer that over their current contentious relationship. "Good try, Fontaine, but it isn't going to happen. Why don't you and Tina make it easy on yourselves and sell out? I'll give you an excellent price."

"Not interested."

Sev shrugged. "I didn't think so, but it was worth a try." He hesitated. "Will you talk to Tina?"

Kurt released his breath in a rough sigh. "Yeah, I'll talk to her. I don't expect it'll change anything. But I will encourage her not to take her anger out on Francesca."

"I'm the one at fault. Tell her to keep me in the crosshairs where I belong, and we'll all do just fine."

With an abrupt nod, Kurt turned and walked away. Sev had no idea whether his plan stood a chance in hell of success. For Francesca's sake, he had to try. She deserved an opportunity to get to know her father, but because he'd been so focused on Dantes and his plans for the business, he'd stolen that opportunity from her. No. Not just stolen. He'd effectively annihilated any chance of it ever happening. If he could restore that much, maybe, just maybe, he could live with the guilt he felt over the rest.

Sev went after Francesca, not in the least surprised to find she'd retreated to the balcony off the ballroom. It was where they'd first met and he struggled not to read anything into her choice. She stood by the railing, her back to him. He could tell she sensed him the instant he appeared in the doorway, her awareness betrayed by the mantle of stillness that settled over her.

He approached. "I'm sorry to spring that engagement ring on you, sweetheart."

"Have you lost your mind?" She threw the question over her shoulder without turning. "What in the world were you thinking?"

"That I was Nicolò, I guess."

That did prompt her to swing around. "This was Nicolò's idea?"

"Hell, no. I get all the credit for this one." Sev scrubbed his hand across his jaw. "Or should I say blame? I just meant, it's the sort of crazy scheme he'd have come up with."

"I don't understand. Why would you do such a thing?"

He shrugged. "I had to try and fix the problem somehow."

"Because that's your job. To fix things." It wasn't a question.

"It always has been," he answered simply. "Since the day my father died, I'm all that stood between Dantes succeeding or going under."

"Well, I'm not some business you have to rebuild. You don't have to fix things for me," she insisted. "I've been taking care of myself for a very long time now. I don't need you to step in and assume the job at this late date."

Strongly stated. Maybe a bit too strongly. "Just out of curiosity . . ." He cocked his head to one side. "Have you ever needed anyone since you turned eighteen?"

He caught the faintest of quivers before she stiffened her chin. "No."

He lowered his voice to a caress. "Or should I ask, have you ever wanted anyone?"

"Don't do this," she whispered. "It's not fair. I want permanence, not temporary."

"Not a string of foster homes."

She conceded the accuracy of his observation with a small nod. "Growing up I always felt I had to change who I was so I'd fit in, that being myself wasn't good enough. I refuse to do that any longer. I won't pretend to be something or someone I'm not, not any longer." She tugged at the ring he'd given her. "This doesn't belong on my finger. Not until it's the real thing."

He stopped her before she could remove it, closing his hand over hers. "Leave it there for the time being. I forced you to work for me. Caused dissension for you both at Timeless and at Dantes. The ring will help protect you. It may even right a few wrongs."

She hesitated. "What's the point? It has to come off sometime."

"But not yet." Not until he'd had time to come up with a resolution to their problems. "Listen to me, honey. There's a very good possibility that our engagement will give you the opportunity to reestablish a relationship with the Fontaines. They're less likely to blame you for leaving them if they believe I forced the issue. They could be part of your life again. You might not see your father as often as you would if you still worked for TH. But at least they won't be angry with you any longer."

"Do you really think so?"

Stark longing filled her expression, ripping him apart. "Give it a chance and see," he suggested roughly.

She teetered on the edge of temptation. "How long do you expect me to keep up this charade?"

"For as long as it takes."

"But it's a lie," Francesca protested.

"Is it?"

A single tug had their bodies colliding in the sweetest of impacts. Sev wrapped his arms around her. The mere touch of her body fomented a reaction unlike anything he'd ever felt with another woman. He'd assumed the acuteness of their passion would ease after a few weeks, that eventually they'd both become sated and the sexual intensity would diminish. It hadn't, and from his perspective, neither of them was close to sated.

A tremor swept through her, one so slight he'd have missed it if they hadn't been fused together from hip to shoulder. He recognized that shiver, felt it each time he pulled her into his arms, and it never failed to excite him. It betrayed a sensual helplessness, one reserved only for him. It whispered her secret to him, teased him with the knowledge that with one touch, her defenses would fall before his advance.

"Let me in, sweetheart."

She gripped his shoulders, pushing even as she yielded. "We're through. Whatever existed between us is over. It ended the minute you forced me into this devil's bargain with you. Putting a ring on my finger to protect me doesn't change that. You put business ahead of our relationship and that's the end of anything personal."

"You know that isn't true."

He swept a hand from the base of her spine to the nape of her neck. Her shiver became a shudder. The give of her body ripened into a heated abandonment, one that silently incited him to deepen their embrace. She wanted him.

She might resist it, but nothing could stop the combustible reaction whenever they touched. Not personal preference. Not logic or intellect. Not even her hurt and anger at the hideous position in which he'd put her.

The dragon's breath of The Inferno incinerated both reason and intellect, and left behind a single urge. To mate. To step into the fire of that joining and allow the flames to consume them.

He lowered his head, his mouth hovering above hers so their breath became one. "I wish this weren't happening when it's clear you don't want it. I wish I could do what you ask and let you go. But I can't."

"You don't have any choice," she asserted. "Do you really think that after all you've done I could ever trust you again?"

"I'm not asking for your trust."

"Just me in your bed."

He didn't bother denying the truth. "Yes, I want you there. Or here. Or anywhere I can have you. Any way you'll allow it."

He closed the final gap between them and sank into her mouth. He heard her sigh of pleasure. Felt it. Drank it inward. Their lips molded, shaping themselves one to the other, before parting. Her breathing grew ragged. Or maybe it was his. More. The insistent demand sounded in his head, so clear and sharp he almost thought he'd said it aloud. And maybe he did, because she reared back, breaking the kiss almost as soon as it began.

She turned her head a fraction to avoid any risk of their lips colliding again. "Making love to you is too intimate. It leaves me too vulnerable," she told him with devastating frankness, the stark pain underscoring her words ripping through him. "I can't open myself to you if I don't trust you."

"We'll find a way to make this work," he insisted.

He'd said the wrong thing. Instantly, she ripped free of his embrace. "There's only one way that's possible. I can work for you or I can sleep with you. But I refuse to do both. It's your choice, Sev."

She gazed at him and he could see the burgeoning hope in the inky darkness, a hope he had no option but to crush. "I believe we've already had this conversation. You work for Dantes."

He forced himself not to flinch at the acrid disillusionment that shattered the last of her hope. Her chin shot up and she embraced her fury. God, she was even more gorgeous, if that were possible, filled with righteous indignation and feminine power.

"You're the consummate businessman to the bitter end, aren't you, Sev?" she said bitterly. "No matter who gets in your way or how many get hurt."

He opened the door a crack so she could see inside. "There's never been any other choice for me. My family has always depended on me to be the ruthless one."

"I'm not in your way, Sev."

He inclined his head. "Not anymore. You need to understand, sweetheart, that my family still depends on me to make the hard decisions. If I don't make them, if I'm too weak to make them, I put Dantes at risk again."

"Fine. Now you've made one more hard decision. You've chosen Dantes over our relationship." She stepped back. "Just don't expect me to reward you for that decision."

He dared to touch her a final time. He scraped his knuckles along the curve of her cheek and pretended not to see her flinch. "I'm sure that's your intention now. But you will be back in my bed. There won't be any other choice." He smiled, a painful pull of his mouth. "For either of us."

Francesca twisted the engagement ring she'd worn for the past ten days, the fire diamond flashing fiercely up at her. It still surprised to discover it decorating her finger. "Who all will be at your grandparents' house for dinner?" she asked Sev.

He shot her a quick glance of reassurance, which dashed any hopes that he hadn't picked up on her nervousness. "Just Nonna, Primo, and my brothers this time around. I'll save the rest of the family for another occasion."

"Oh." She started to twist her hands together again, but the fire diamond stopped her, flashing an additional message of reassurance. To her amusement, it worked and she found herself relaxing despite herself. "Does your family get together often?" she asked, honestly curious.

"Once a month without fail."

"Do they know our engagement isn't real?"

"It is real. For now. As far as my family's concerned, you and I are engaged," he warned. "I'd appreciate it if you wouldn't disabuse them of that notion."

Her brows pulled together. "And how did you explain the suddenness of it? Or the fact that I used to work at TH and now work for you?"

"Easy. I told them we had no choice. It was The Inferno." He shrugged. "I didn't need any other explanation after that."

She caught her bottom lip between her teeth. So much for relaxing. Whenever she'd been sent to a new foster home, that first meeting always proved the most difficult for her. Most of the time she walked into situations where the other foster children, or her foster parents' natural children, had already formed tight family units. Sure, they always welcomed her. At first. But she dreaded those early days of adjustment, hovering on the outside of their too jovial camaraderie as she tried to figure out how to best fit in. What hole she could fill, regardless of whether the fit felt comfortable.

This time around they all believed her madly in love with Sev. How could she possibly convince them of that? "I don't think I can pull this off."

"Don't worry about it," he told her softly. "We won't stay long if you're not enjoying yourself."

"I'll be fine." And she would. She could handle the situation. After all, she wasn't a lost child any longer. And if she'd learned nothing else during those formative years, she'd learned how to fake it.

To her delight, she discovered she didn't have to fake anything. From the moment she and Sev walked in the door, the Dantes welcomed her with open arms. Primo and Nonna both gave her exuberant hugs, exclaiming in pleasure over her choice of engagement ring.

"It's a stunning design," Francesca complimented Primo with utter sincerity. "I told Sev how envious I am that it isn't my own creation."

"I am honored," he said, clearly moved. "And I am even more honored that you have chosen this particular ring to wear for as many years as God blesses your marriage."

The breath caught in her lungs, the weight of his words pressing down on her. "Thank you," she managed to answer, shooting Sev a look of clear desperation.

He responded by lifting her left hand to his mouth in a move that should have come across as hackneyed. Instead it struck her as unbelievably endearing. Her throat closed as his gaze linked with hers. And just like that, in front of all the Dantes, The Inferno struck and she totally melted.

Nonna dabbed at her eyes and smiled at Primo reminiscently. Then she clapped her hands together, scolding in Italian. As one, the Dante men shuffled toward the kitchen, where they switched from English to Italian. Sev left last.

He ran his thumb along the curve of her bottom lip. "You okay?" he asked quietly.

She blew out her breath in a sigh, murmuring in an undertone, "Well, I don't think we have to worry about whether or not they believe our engagement is real."

He bent and captured her mouth, no doubt because he knew she didn't dare protest. Not that protesting occurred to her until long after he'd released her. "No, we don't."

Nonna grinned as she watched their parting. "It is good, what you have. Special."

"I think complicated might be a more accurate description."

Nonna nodded in agreement. "With Dante men, it can be nothing less." She gathered Francesca's hand in hers. "He needs you, that one. Oh, you may look at him and wonder. He is so strong. So hard-nosed. He is quite capable of standing on his own. But he has had to be. He has had no choice but to take the one path open to him. Anything else would have meant disaster for his family."

"Because—" Francesca broke off, realizing it might not be politic to mention her son's poor business skills had almost destroyed the business her husband built.

Nonna nodded. "You are tactful. I appreciate that. But what you are thinking is true. Dominic almost destroyed Dantes." Lines of grief couldn't detract from a face still handsome despite the weight of her years. "If not for Severo, Dantes would be no more."

"It couldn't have been easy for him."

"It was more than difficult. The decisions he has made . . ." Nonna shook her head. "Any man would find them near to impossible. But at so young an age, so soon after the death of his mother and father?" She clicked her tongue in distress.

"You're saying he had to be ruthless." As he'd proven to her on more than one occasion these past weeks.

"Yes." Nonna closed her eyes and whispered a silent prayer. Then she looked at Francesca, joy replacing her sorrow. "But then he found you. He needs you, *ciccina*. You soften him. And after all that has been forced on him, all the horrible choices, you give him peace. Best of all, you give him The Inferno."

With a grateful smile, she linked arms with Francesca and urged her toward the kitchen. It troubled Francesca to see the situation from Sev's side of the fence. She didn't want to sympathize with all he'd been through.

Worse, rather than fading, her physical and emotional response toward him grew progressively stronger with each passing day.

Considering all that stood between them, it would make life easier if it would just go away. She entered the kitchen and spared him a swift look, confirming those feelings weren't going anywhere anytime soon.

To her surprise, she spotted Primo at the stove, commandeering the burners like an admiral overseeing his fleet, while the Dante men moved in practiced synchronicity, taking care of all the domestic chores in preparation for the meal.

Her surprise must have shown because Nonna grinned. "This is my night off. It is a Dante tradition," she explained, gesturing toward her grandchildren. "They take care of me on family day."

"I like that." Francesca's eyes narrowed in suspicion. "They do dishes, too, right? You don't get stuck with those?"

"No, no." She gave a broad wink. "I am too clever for that. Here. You take Gianna's seat next to me. She's in *L'Italia*. Visiting *famiglia* with her parents and brothers. You will meet them next time."

Assuming there was a next time, Francesca almost said, before catching back the words at the last second. Fortunately, dinner came together just then and the Dante men descended on the table like they hadn't eaten in a month. After grace, conversation exploded, for the most part in English, occasionally in Italian, as a bewildering array of dishes passed back and forth.

The choices were endless. Marinated calamari vied with *panzanella*. Cannellini beans cooked with garlic, olive oil and sage competed with stuffed tomatoes. Then the main dishes marched around the table. Chicken Marsala with red peppers, tortellini, pasta with a variety of sauces.

"Save room for dessert," Sev warned as he piled her food high.

She shook her head at the overloaded plate. "I can serve myself, you know."

He gave her a look a shade too innocent. "I just wanted to make sure you try a bit of everything."

She knew him too well to buy into that one. "I think you want to stuff me full of carbs so my brain goes to sleep."

"Now why would I want to do that?" But his mouth twitched, giving him away.

"So I can't think fast enough to argue with you."

He grinned. "But, *cara*, I love arguing with you."

A liquid warmth swept through her again at the teeny-tiny accent that crept through his words. No doubt the setting contributed to it, and the fact that he constantly switched back and forth between English and Italian.

"Ho-ho. What a liar you are," Nonna corrected in Italian. "It is not the arguing you love. It is the making up afterward."

"Well . . ." Francesca offered judiciously. "He does excel at both."

Silence descended over the table. *"Parlate italiano?"* Nonna demanded in astonishment. "And why did you not tell us this?"

Francesca grinned. "How would I know what you were all saying about me if I admitted I spoke Italian?"

Delighted laughter rang out as they all bombarded her with questions in rapid-fire succession. Primo rapped his knuckles in an effort to regain control. Instantly, silence descended. "I will ask the questions at my own table, if you do not mind," he informed his grandsons. Eyes identical to Sev's fixed her with uncomfortable shrewdness. "You have Italian relatives? This is why you learned Italian?" he asked.

She shook her head. "As far as I'm aware I'm not of Italian descent." A shadow of regret came and went. "I'm afraid I don't know much about my ancestors, so anything's possible, I suppose."

She caught a hint of compassion in Primo's expression, though he didn't allow it to color his voice. "Then why?" he asked. "Why did you learn Italian?"

"Because it's always been my dream to work at Dantes," she admitted. "It made sense to learn the language." A subtle shift in attitude occurred after her confession, one that left her somewhat puzzled.

"Figured it out yet?" Sev asked softly.

Her gaze jerked up to meet his. "Figured what out?"

"You'll get there." He gave her a small wedge of *panforte*, a traditional Tuscan dessert filled with nuts, fruit and a hint of chocolate, serving her a cup of strong coffee to accompany it.

"Do you mean . . . ?" She glanced around the table, reassured to see that a heated discussion about the best time to expand Dantes raged on, preoccupying the rest of Sev's family. "Do you mean have I worked out the change in your family? The change in their attitude toward me?"

"Almost there," he murmured.

She shrugged. "That's easy enough. It's because they found out I speak Italian. I blend in better."

"Not even close."

Startled, she gave him her full attention. "What? They love me now because I told them I've always wanted to work at Dantes? So what? Lots of people would kill to work for you."

"Nope. Come on, honey. You know. You just refuse to accept the significance of it."

He saw too clearly and it left her far too vulnerable. She returned her fork to her plate, before confessing, "It's because I learned Italian in the hope I'd someday work for Dantes. That I took that extra step."

A slow smile built across his mouth. "I knew you'd get it."

She scanned the table again, realizing that with that simple, painfully honest statement she'd become one of the family, her acceptance into their inner circle absolute. Most important of all, she'd done it by being herself. Even so, the knowledge filled her with guilt. "But it's a lie."

He helped himself to a second slice of *panforte*. "You didn't learn Italian because you wanted to work for me?"

"Not you," she stressed. "Dantes. And not that." She shoved her left hand under his nose. "This. This is a—"

He leaned over and stopped her with a kiss. "We'll discuss that later," he murmured against her mouth. "In the meantime, don't worry.

These things have a way of sorting themselves out."

They lingered over their coffee for another hour before Sev stood and told his family they needed to leave. Hugs were liberally dispensed before they made it out the door. The instant they slid into the car, she returned to the concern uppermost on her mind.

"Can't we tell your family the truth? I really like them, and I'd rather not lie to them."

"We're not lying to them. We are engaged."

"You know what I mean." Impatience edged her voice. "They think we're getting married."

"That might prove a problem at some point," he conceded. "But not today."

They both fell silent until he pulled up outside her apartment complex. After curbing the wheels to keep them from rolling downhill, he threw the car in Park and shut off the engine. A gentle rain tapped against the windshield and blocked out everything but a watery blur of city lights.

"Have you really always wanted to work at Dantes?" he asked.

"Yes."

"Then you've achieved your dream. Is a temporary engagement to me so high a price to pay for that dream?"

"No." She touched her engagement ring in an increasingly familiar gesture. "But what I've done to the Fontaines is far too high a price for any dream."

"You need to trust me. It's all going to work out. It may not be a perfect solution. Compromise will be involved. But it's going to work out."

"Because you say so?"

"Because I intend to make it so."

He cupped her face and drew her close. At the first brush of his mouth against hers, every thought evaporated from her head. The Fontaines. The Dante clan. Work pressures. They all slipped away beneath the heat of his taking. He played with her mouth, offering light, teasing kisses. But it only took her tiny moan of pleasure for it to transform into something more. Something deep and sensual and unbearably desperate. Passion exploded, fogging the windows and ripping apart both intent and intention. It needed to stop before stopping became an impossibility.

"You don't play fair," she protested, struggling to draw breath.

"It doesn't pay to play fair." He eyed her in open amusement. "What it does is give me what I want most."

"And what's that?" she couldn't resist asking.

"You." He lifted an eyebrow. "Invite me in and put us both out of our misery."

Did he think it would be that easy to recover the ground they'd lost? She swallowed a groan. Maybe if their embrace had continued for another few minutes, though she'd never admit as much to Sev. But it hadn't, and she still found enough self-possession—*somewhere,* if she looked around hard enough—to stand firm in her resolve not to tumble back into his bed.

"No, I'm not inviting you in." She gave him her sweetest smile. "I don't play fair, either. As far as I'm concerned, you can sit here and suffer for your sins."

"But not for much longer," he said.

Or was it a warning?

Chapter Nine

Francesca flipped through her sketchpad and experienced a sense of accomplishment unlike anything she'd ever felt before. She'd worked on the creations contained on these pages for most of her life.

It hadn't been her first glimpse of the sparkle and glitter of gemstones that had drawn her to jewelry design. Sure, she loved the beauty of them. And she loved the endless ideas that danced through her imagination, ideas for how to combine the different gemstones into stunning patterns. But that hadn't been what snagged her heart.

From the moment she'd understood the true symbolism of a wedding ring and what it stood for . . . From the instant she realized what her mother never experienced, and no doubt longed to share with the man she loved, Francesca had been drawn to create the dream. And now she had.

She studied her designs one last time, thrilled that she'd completed what she'd set out to achieve all those years ago. She'd given birth to something beyond her wildest expectations and, ironically, she owed it all to Severo Dante. Somehow, at some point, he'd crept into her heart and given her the final spark of inspiration she'd needed to bring her designs to life.

Tears filled her eyes and she shook her head with a smile. How ridiculous to get all weepy over a bunch of drawings. She hadn't even completed a mockup of them, yet. Not that it mattered. She knew how the finished product would look. She even knew how they could market the collection. An entire campaign existed between the covers of her sketchpad, a campaign that would relaunch Dantes into a full line of women's jewelry, should that possibility interest them.

Flipping her pad closed, she locked it away just as her studio door banged open. Tina stood there, looking more devastated than Francesca had ever seen her.

"Tina? What's wrong?" Francesca asked, half-rising. "What's happened?"

"Is it true?" Tina slammed the door closed behind her, closeting them together in the room. "All this time I thought you were the innocent in all this. That Dante had you completely snowed. I actually thought maybe we could work things out between us. But now I'm not so sure."

A sick suspicion clawed at Francesca's stomach. "What are you talking about?"

"I'm talking about my husband." Tina's mouth twisted. "Or should I say . . . your father."

Francesca felt every scrap of color drain from her face and she sank back into her chair. "You can't be serious. I'm not—"

Tina cut her off with a swipe of her hand. "Don't. At least have the decency not to lie to me." Her heels pounded out a succession of hard staccato raps as she crossed the room. "I have the evidence."

"How?"

"That's not important." She reached the edge of the desk and Francesca could see the wild pain lurking in the older woman's eyes. "You lied to me. To Kurt."

"Only about my connection to him. Only that, I swear."

A wild laugh ripped loose. "Only that? Only?"

How could she explain? "I just wanted to get to know him. From a distance," Francesca emphasized. "I never planned to tell either of you the truth."

Fury ignited. "What were you waiting for? To worm your way into our good graces and then spring it on us? Hope Kurt was smitten enough with the idea of having a daughter that he'd give you a piece of my business?" She slammed her palms on Francesca's desk. *"My* business. Not Kurt's. He may keep the production end of things afloat, but I'm the creative force behind Timeless Heirlooms."

Francesca shook her head. "You don't understand. I'd never do anything to cause trouble for you two." Guilt overwhelmed her. She never should have applied for a job at TH. Never should have put her own selfish needs ahead of respecting the sanctity of her father's marriage. "I just wanted to get to know my father," she confessed miserably. "I never planned to tell either of you who I was. Please, Tina. This isn't Kurt's fault."

"I'm well aware of whose fault this is." She stabbed a finger at Francesca. *"Yours.* You chose to come into our life. You chose to become involved with Severo Dante. You ruined my marriage."

"Ruined?" Francesca shot to her feet. "No, Tina. Don't walk out on Kurt. Not because of me."

"I can add. Better yet, I can subtract. According to our personnel records, you're twenty-six. That means Kurt and I were married three years when he—" She broke off, clearly softened the description she'd been about to use. "When he had an affair with your mother."

"It was a long time ago, Tina. All anyone has to do is look at him to know he's crazy in love with you." Francesca jettisoned every scrap of pride to plead on Kurt's behalf. "After thirty years of marriage, surely that counts for something?"

"Maybe it would have, if not for you. But every time I see you, every time I hear your name or see your designs, it's a slap in the face. Living proof of my husband's infidelity." Tina spun around and stalked to the door. Once there, she paused. "Oh, and by the way? You can thank your fiancé for clueing me in to your true identity. It would seem he'll do anything to get his hands on TH. Even destroy my marriage."

Sev sat behind his desk, papers strewn across the thick glass surface. Some were preliminary jewelry designs, others financial statements from the various international branches, still others proposals for expansion. All of the reports demanded his immediate attention.

A knock sounded at his door just as he reached for the first report. Before he could respond, Francesca entered the room. She shut the door behind her with a tad too much emphasis, warning of her less than stellar mood.

"How could you?" she demanded.

He stilled, studying her through narrowed eyes. "Clichéd, but intriguing nonetheless. Dare I ask, how could I what?"

"Tina knows. Tina knows I'm Kurt's daughter. There's only one person who could have told her."

"I gather that's where I come in." He leaned back in his chair, reaching for calm. For some reason that only served to push her anger to greater heights.

"Don't," she warned sharply. "Don't play with me."

"I'd love to play with you, though not about this." He gave her a level look. "Honey, I haven't broken my promise to you. The only contact I've had with Tina is to up my offer for Timeless Heirlooms."

Francesca shook her head. "You don't get it. You—or one of your brothers—are the only ones who could have told her. No one else knows."

He smiled at that, which might have been a mistake judging by the flash of fury that glittered in her dark eyes. "Someone must know, otherwise we wouldn't have uncovered the information in the first place."

She slowly shook her head. "I hired a private investigator four years ago to find my father. He couldn't. But he did find an old friend of my mother's and she's the one who revealed my father's identity. I never told anyone, not even the PI. So unless someone tracked this woman down and forced her to talk, I have trouble believing the leak came from her."

That caught him by surprise. Shoving back his chair, he stood and circled his desk. Cupping her elbow, he drew her over to the sitting area on the far side of the room. "Are you certain she didn't tell anyone else?"

"I can't be positive." She perched on the edge of the couch and he sat next to her, too close judging by the tide of awareness that washed through her. She struggled to hide her dismay by directing it toward anger. "But I find it highly unlikely she'd call Tina out of the blue and just hand over that information. It doesn't make any sense."

He analyzed what she'd said, looking for alternate explanations. "What about your foster parents? Is it possible they had that information?"

"Not a chance. They'd have turned Kurt's name over to the state to force him to pay child support." She leveled him with a censorious look. "How did you find out about Kurt? Who in your organization knows the truth?"

"We hired a private investigator to check you out," he admitted.

She couldn't prevent the accusation. "You've had me investigated?"

"We had all of TH's designers investigated as a matter of course." He held up a hand to ward off her indignation. "Listen, I'll contact the investigator and ascertain how he came across the information. All I can tell you is that I didn't betray your secret to Tina. Nor did any of my brothers."

She surged to her feet and paced across his office. "This is going to destroy the Fontaines' marriage."

"Maybe. Maybe not." Though, privately, he'd rate it closer to probable, edging toward definite.

"If it does, you'll be able to pick up TH for a song."

He absorbed the accusation. "Which automatically makes me guilty?"

She spun to face him. "Tina claimed you told her. And it makes sense. Who else profits from revealing the truth to her?"

He shrugged. "As far as I know, no one."

"You're not helping yourself." Frustration riddled her expression. "You realize that, don't you?"

"I realize that nothing I say will change your mind. I also realize you don't trust me."

"How could I? Why would I?" She thrust her fingers through her hair, tumbling the curls into delicious disarray. "Since the minute we met you've done nothing to inspire that trust."

That got to him, shaving some of the calm from his temper. "Our nights together didn't inspire trust? Our time together hasn't proven the sort of man I am?"

Tears welled in her eyes again. "Those nights meant everything to me, more than they could have meant to you or you'd never have blackmailed me. You'd never have forced me to betray the Fontaines and work for you."

He climbed to his feet to give weight to his words. "I intend to return Dantes to its position as an international powerhouse, no matter what sort of sacrifices that requires. I made that fact crystal clear to you right from the start. I will recover every last subsidiary I was forced to sell off when I assumed the reins of this company. And that includes TH."

She tugged off his engagement ring and held it out. "Take this. I refuse to wear it a minute longer."

He simply shook his head. "That's not happening. If we break our engagement so soon after we announce it, your life within the jewelry world will become unbearable." He held up his hand to stem her protest. "As my fiancée, you have the Dante name to protect you. No one will dare say a word about you, your talent, or where you choose to work. Nor will anyone dare say anything should Tina decide to be indiscreet."

Her mouth trembled. "You think she'll tell people I'm Kurt's daughter? You think she'll publicly blame me for TH's demise?"

"A woman that angry is capable of anything. There's no telling what she'll do."

Francesca made a swift recovery, one that impressed the hell out of him. "I don't care about any of that. Let people talk. Let Tina do her worst. Let the world assume whatever they want."

"Right. And maybe you could handle the public fallout. Damned if you don't seem determined to try. But I have Dantes to consider. Becoming engaged one day and ending it only weeks later is not the image I want to project to the general public, my suppliers, or my associates and competitors."

"Then you never should have come up with this scheme."

"Point taken, but it's a little late for that." He offered a wry smile. "When I came up with the idea, my only consideration was you and trying to salvage your relationship with the Fontaines. That's what I get for thinking like Nicolò."

For an endless moment she wavered between acceptance and rejection. To his profound relief, she released her breath in a sigh of reluctant agreement. "How long? How long do we have to keep up the pretense?"

"For as long as it takes." He ran his hands up and down her arms, picking up on the slight shiver she couldn't quite suppress. "Give it time, sweetheart. Is it really so bad being engaged to me? You liked my family, didn't you?"

Once again, he'd said the wrong thing. Her eyes darkened in distress. "I don't want to fall in love with them."

He could guess why. "Because it hurts too much when it ends and you're forced to walk away."

She didn't deny it. Instead she changed the subject. "What about the Fontaines? You have to promise me you won't take advantage of this latest wrinkle. You have to promise me you're still going to pay full price for TH, even if their marriage falls apart."

He refused to be anything other than straight with her. "If they offer me a good deal, I'm not going to turn it down."

Maybe he shouldn't have been quite that straight. She pulled back and glared. "We have a contract. You have to pay them full price for their business. And I intend to make sure you stick to that agreement."

"Our contract states I'm to pay fair market value. That's what I intend to pay and not a penny more."

"Even if the fair market value drops because Kurt and Tina divorce?"

"Fair. Market. Value," he repeated succinctly.

She stilled and something drifted across her expression, something that had the businessman in him going on red alert. Then she gave a careless shrug. "If that's the best you're willing to do, I guess I have no choice but to accept it, do I?"

He stared at her through narrowed eyes. "That's precisely what I expect you to do, since that's precisely what the contract calls for."

She turned to leave his office without further argument, which worried him all the more. Hell. No question about it. She was up to something, and he suspected he wouldn't like whatever scheme she was busily hatching.

Later that evening, Francesca stood outside Sev's apartment building, her head bent against the rain, soaked to the skin from an unexpected shower. Why had he demanded she come by tonight of all nights? she wondered in despair. Maybe if she hadn't gotten together with Kurt she wouldn't be finding this so difficult. But when she'd suggested waiting until morning to show Sev her latest designs, he'd insisted that he needed to see them tonight.

She shivered uncontrollably, wanting nothing more than to crawl into her bathtub at home and have a long, hot soak in conjunction with an even longer cry. Swiping the dampness from her cheeks—rain, she attempted to reassure herself, not tears—she rode the elevator to the top floor of Sev's apartment building and applied fist to door.

It opened almost immediately. "What the hell?" Sev took one look at her and swept her across the threshold and into his apartment, ignoring her disjointed protests about dripping all over his hardwood floors. "I don't give a flying f—" He tempered the expression. "A flying fig about the damn floors. I care about you. What the hell's happened? Are you all right?"

"I'm wet." She trembled and held out the packet of designs. "Maybe cold, too. I'm shaking so hard it's sort of tough to tell."

He snatched the designs from her hand and tossed them aside. The packet hit the floor and skidded under an antique coat closet. Then he unceremoniously swept her into his arms and carried her into the master bathroom. She couldn't rouse herself enough to fight him when he stripped first her, and then himself, and pulled them both into the glassed-in shower stall. He turned the jets on high and she stood docilely beneath the blazing-hot torrent and let the water wash away all emotion.

"What happened?" he asked again, more gently this time.

She didn't even realize she spoke until she heard her voice echoing against the tile. "He didn't want me, Sev. My father. He agreed to meet me tonight and then sent me away. He said he was sorry. Sorry!" She covered her face with her hands as she fought for control. "Sorry he had an affair with my mother. Sorry she became pregnant. Sorry Tina found out the truth. He said he couldn't see me ever again."

"He's a fool."

She dropped her hands and stared up at Sev. "What did I do? What did I do wrong?"

He hugged her fiercely. "You didn't do anything wrong. Not a damn thing. It's them, honey. Something's wrong with them. But you have me and you have the rest of the Dantes. And they flat-out adore you." A raw ferocity coated his words. "We'll be your family from now on."

"When they find out we're not really engaged, they won't want me, either," she felt obligated to point out, tears welling anew.

"They will. I promise." He continued to hold her close while the water poured down on them. "Easy, sweetheart. Let it all out. You'll feel better if you do."

Let what out? Didn't he understand? She felt dead inside. Her father rejected her. She couldn't say why she cared so much. After all, what did one more rejection matter after so many?

At long last, Sev shut off the water and left her dripping, naked and alone, in the middle of the tile floor. An instant later he reappeared with an armload of towels. He slung one around his waist and dropped another on her head, before swathing her from shoulders to knees in a third. Then he proceeded to rub her down with a briskness that caused her skin to glow.

"What are you doing?" she asked, emotional exhaustion leaving her only mildly curious.

"You're in shock. I need to get you warm."

She peered at him from beneath the towel. "I'm not shocked. I'm not even surprised. I knew what would happen if Kurt and Tina found out the truth about me."

He knelt at her feet, drying her with an impersonal touch that had her responding in far too personal a way. "You'd be rejected, just as you've been rejected so many times before."

She shrugged, admitting, "I'm sort of used to it."

"Yeah, I know. That's what kills me."

"Don't let it bother you. It doesn't bother me. Not anymore."

"I shouldn't ask. But I will." He rocked back on his heels and stared up at her, his face set in grim lines. "Why doesn't it bother you anymore?"

She spoke slowly, as though to a backward child. "Because I can't feel." Sheesh. Didn't he get it? "When you can't feel, it doesn't hurt."

For some reason that made him swear. When he'd run out of invectives, he planted a hand low on her back and ushered her from the bathroom. "I don't know about you, but I could use a drink."

"Several, I think."

"Hmm. And something to eat."

Ten minutes later, she was curled up on the floor in front of a fire, dining on a selection of imported cheese and crackers while sipping the smoothest single-malt whiskey she'd ever tasted. Sev lounged beside her, a towel still knotted at his waist. She woke to her surroundings sufficiently to admire the miles of toned muscle rising above the soft white fleece.

Lord help her, but he was the most gorgeous man she'd ever seen. He hadn't bothered to brush his hair, simply slicked it back from his face so it clung damply to the back of his neck in heavy, dark waves. His features reminded her somewhat of Primo, with the same rugged handsomeness and noble bearing. And, of course, the same stunning eye color. But the rest . . . Oh, my. The rest was pure Severo Dante.

She buried her nose in the crystal tumbler and took a quick sip. Unable to help herself, she peeked at him from over the rim. Memories from their nights together came storming back. They'd made love right here in front of the fire at least a half-dozen times. Several more times on the couch behind them when they'd been too impatient to traverse the short distance from there to the bedroom. Most nights she shared with him, a pathway appeared, one strewn with clothes spreading from front door to bed.

How she enjoyed those moments, especially when she wrestled him free of that last article of clothing. He had the most incredible body, lean and graceful, yet powerful enough to lift her with ease, which he often did, then tip her onto silken sheets and cover her with that endless length of potent masculinity.

She drained the last of the whiskey and set the glass aside. "I need you to do me a favor," she informed him.

"If I can."

"Oh, you can." The only question was . . . Would he? "I want you to make love to me. I want to feel something again."

He studied her for a long, silent moment and she could see him preparing a list of excuses. She was too vulnerable. He didn't want to take advantage of her. There were still so many issues unresolved between them. But something in her gaze, or perhaps it was something buried deep in his heart, must have convinced him otherwise.

Instead of turning her down, he tugged the towel free of her hair and tossed it aside before pulling her onto his lap and thrusting his hands deep into her damp curls. Turning her to fully face him, her knees settling on either side of his hips, he closed his mouth over hers in a kiss hot enough to leave scorch marks. She opened for him, welcoming him home. The duel was short and sweet, a battle for supremacy that neither lost, yet both won.

"Do you feel that?" he asked.

The question slid from his mouth to hers and she laughed softly in response. "I'm not sure. I might have noticed a slight tingle."

His eyes narrowed. "Slight tingle? Slight?"

She blinked with patently false innocence and wiggled her bottom in a provocative motion against him. "Very slight."

"Let's see what we can do about that."

He flipped her off his lap and onto her back. Firelight lapped over his determined face and caught in his eyes, causing the gold to burn like wildfire. She missed this. Missed seeing his abandoned reaction whenever they touched. Missed the romantic soul that blunted the contours of his male sexuality. Missed opening to him—physically and emotionally—in the darkest hours of the night and sharing all she hid within her heart. And having him share what he kept locked away in his. But most of all, she missed this. The intimacy. The passion. Possessing and being possessed.

He kissed her again. Deeper. More thoroughly. He worshiped her with mouth and tongue until she went mindless with pleasure. "Tell me you feel that," he demanded.

She groaned. "A tickle. Barely a tickle."

"Right. That's it."

Uh-oh. Annoyed obstinance if ever she heard it. He kissed a path downward, mixing the gentle caresses with love nips that had her toes curling into knots. He ripped the towel open and bared her to a combination of firelight and heated gaze. He shot her one last lingering look before applying himself to his appointed task.

He glided his hands along the sides of her breasts, using just the very tips of his fingers so he barely connected with her skin. She shivered at the sensation, shocked that so light a touch could provoke such a strong reaction. She bit back a cry, forcing herself to remain silent, even though it just might kill her. No. *Definitely* would kill her.

Around he circled, edging ever closer to the pebbled tips of her breasts. She fought with every ounce of self-possession to keep from begging him to take her, almost shooting off the plush carpet when his teeth closed over her nipple and tugged.

If she'd ever questioned The Inferno before, she didn't now. It erupted, low in her belly, spilling over like molten lava. It liquefied everything in its path as it began an onslaught of hunger so deep and all-consuming, she literally shook with the effort to contain it.

He moved lower, touching her belly with his fingers and mouth. Lower. Brushing the nest of curls that protected her feminine core. Lower. Took the heart of her with his mouth. She went deaf and blind as her climax ripped her apart. She fought to draw air into lungs squeezed breathless, barely aware that Sev had left her side.

She still hadn't recovered when he returned, carefully protected, and settled between her thighs. "Do you feel alive now? Do you feel wanted?"

Sensations toppled one on top of another, so intense she couldn't process them all. *"Sev . . ."* His name escaped in a husky cry, half concession, half demand. "Pleaseohpleaseohplease."

He probed inward, a teasing, swirling movement. "Do you feel this?"

"Yes." She moaned as he slid deep, driving all the way home. "I'm definitely feeling something I never have before."

She wrapped her legs around his waist and held on. She'd never felt more alive. Never felt more wanted or cherished. Never belonged with anyone as she did with Sev in this moment. Her climax approached again, every bit as powerful as before. Only this time he joined her. To her amazement, it didn't rip or shred, but melded, uniting them together in something so different, so special, she couldn't at first find the word to name it. And then it came to her and in doing so, overwhelmed her with the devastating knowledge.

In that brief moment, she no longer stood on the outside looking in. Love opened the door and she flew inside.

Chapter Ten

Morning found Sev in bed wrapped around Francesca in a complicated tangle of arms and legs. He had a vague recollection of scraping her boneless body off the carpet and tossing her over his shoulder before staggering to the bedroom. Or maybe they'd just crawled here.

She stirred within his embrace and flopped onto her back with a groan. He smiled at the sight. She'd gone to bed with damp hair and now it surrounded her head like a fluffy halo. Something told him she wouldn't appreciate her appearance anywhere near as much as he did.

His smile faded as a new and unfamiliar realization took hold. Last night their relationship had changed, a change that went way beyond what it had been before, on either the work front or as former lovers. Somehow, it had shifted them into an entirely new realm, a realm neither of them anticipated.

"Who glued my eyes shut?" She forced one open. "Hey, we're in bed."

"Excellent observation."

"How'd we get here?"

"Beats the hell out of me."

"Maybe I carried you in before I had my wicked way with you. Again."

He grinned. "That's entirely possible."

"Is it just me?" She hesitated, an innate wariness flickering like a warning light. "Or did something peculiar happen to us last night? Even more peculiar than The Inferno, I mean. Although how that's even possible is beyond me."

He framed her face, tracing the delicate bone structure with his fingertips until the shape and texture became as familiar to him as his own. The need to remain in physical contact with her had become an urge he no longer bothered resisting. The Inferno had won.

"I believe we both realized the truth last night," he admitted.

She regarded him with some reservation. "Which is?"

"This isn't going away." He lifted her left hand and studied the engagement ring she wore. The inner fire seemed to erupt from the center of the diamond, fiercer than he'd ever seen it before. "Maybe we should consider making this permanent."

He absorbed her jerk of surprise, felt her heart rate kick up a notch. "Are you serious?"

"I think it's worth discussing, don't you?"

A small smile played at the corners of her mouth. It grew until her entire face radiated with it. "I wouldn't mind," she admitted softly.

On the nightstand table, his cell emitted a soft buzz and Sev swore beneath his breath. "I should have left the damn thing in the other room."

She jackknifed upward and snatched a swift kiss. "Go ahead and take it while I get cleaned up."

"You sure?"

"Positive."

She bounced off the bed and darted into the bathroom. Her muffled shriek of dismay put a grin on his face. Something told him she'd just discovered a mirror. He snagged the phone and took the call. "This better be good," he growled.

"It's Lazz. And it's not good. In fact, it's an effing mess. If you'd bothered to come to work this morning—"

"Get to the point," Sev interrupted.

"Seriously, bro, what the hell are you doing and why aren't you here? There is a fan sitting on my desk cranked to high and you can't believe what just hit it."

"What's wrong?"

"It's Francesca."

Hell. He glanced toward the bathroom. Water ran in the sink and he could hear her humming, the sound light and happy and slightly off-key. "What's the problem?"

"Bloom's rep called. They've decided to go with Timeless."

"Not good, but we knew winning that account would be a long shot. What's it got to do with Francesca?"

At the sound of her name, she appeared in the doorway. She'd tamed her hair, much to his disappointment and, even more disappointing, slipped on one of his shirts. She shot him a questioning look as she rolled up the sleeves, an incandescent happiness pouring off her in waves. After the meeting with Kurt, he didn't think she'd ever find joy again. But she had, and it humbled him that she found it in his arms.

"Francesca's the one who convinced Bloom to go with TH," Lazz said.

Sev shot off the bed. "Not a chance."

"I'm dead serious. Sev, I spoke to the rep. Personally."

He bowed his head and stared at the floor. "She wouldn't have done that. I want you to double-check, Lazz. Triple-check, if that's what it takes. Find out why Bloom's rep would lie to you." And then he looked up, straight into Francesca's eyes. What hovered there in the shadowed darkness had him breaking off with a word he'd never normally use in her presence. He hit the disconnect button. "Lazz doesn't need to triple-check, does he? Bloom's rep told him the truth."

His shirt hung on her, making her appear small and fragile. Or maybe it was the barriers she slammed back in place. He never realized how utterly they enshrouded her until she emerged from their protective folds. Last night she'd bared herself in a way she never had before, not in all the time they'd been together.

Francesca shook her head. "There's no point in his checking again."

"You contacted Juliet Bloom's representative?" At her nod, he hit her with his accusation. "You advised her to go with Timeless."

"Yes. I guaranteed she wouldn't lose if she did so. That it would only benefit her."

He lifted an eyebrow. "Payback, Francesca?" he asked softly.

She tilted her chin to a combative angle and fixed him with a cool, remote gaze that shot his blood pressure straight through the roof. "I prefer to call it insurance."

"Explain," he rapped out.

"Timeless Heirlooms owns the designs that Juliet Bloom is so crazy about. The ones *I* created. She wants to wear them in her next film. Dantes plans to purchase TH, not put them out of business, so Timeless will endure regardless of ownership. Once the company is safely tucked back into the Dantes' fold, you'll receive the continued benefit from having someone of Bloom's caliber as your spokeswoman."

"If we tuck TH back into the Dantes' fold," he corrected tightly. "That's a big, fat effing *if!*"

"You've already assured me it's going to happen, regardless of me, or the Fontaines, or even Juliet Bloom." She lifted an eyebrow. "A lie, Sev?"

His back teeth clamped together. "It's no lie."

"Then what's the problem?" She stepped from the bathroom, wary enough to keep her distance. Smart woman. "All I've done is ensure that you honor the contract we signed and pay the Fontaines a fair price for TH. Now that Bloom's agreed to be the spokeswoman for them, Kurt and Tina will reunite. They'll have no other choice if they want that contract. Knowing Tina as I do, she won't let a little thing like an illegitimate daughter stand in the way of a deal of this magnitude."

"It will, however, make it more difficult for me to acquire TH."

She graciously conceded the point, which had him backing up a step so he wouldn't give in to temptation and throttle her. "But it will happen. And when that day comes, since I work for you, I'm also available to work with Ms. Bloom should she wish to expand the current collection I designed for her. Or I can create a whole new line for her at some point in the future. And if you don't buy out TH, Ms. Bloom will most likely jump ship and become Dantes' spokeswoman, since I now work for you. As far as I can tell, everyone comes out of this a winner."

"Except for you."

That stopped her. About damn time. "What are you talking about?" For the first time a hint of uncertainty crept into her voice.

"I'm talking about the fact that I have the option to either fire you, in which case I'll see to it that you don't work in the industry for the next two years. Or I can transfer you to another office. Either way, Bloom will no longer be your problem."

"Which do you intend to do?"

Francesca asked the question so calmly, if he didn't know better he'd have thought she didn't care. But if he'd learned nothing else about her, he had learned that designing jewelry was as much a part of her as her heart or soul. In fact, it was her soul. He couldn't take that away from her, no matter how badly her actions had hurt him.

And they *had* hurt him. This wasn't about business, anymore. In fact, she'd shown a ruthlessness he could almost admire. A ruthlessness he, himself, had been forced to employ on occasion. No, this had become personal. It felt personal. It felt as though he'd risked opening himself to her, only to have her use what she'd learned to hurt him.

"I believe there's a spot open for you in our New York office. I'll make your transfer effective immediately."

She jerked as though he'd struck her, staring at him for an endless moment with huge, wounded eyes. Without a word, she turned on her heel and moved through the apartment, gathering her possessions. Sev hardened himself as he waited for her to finish and leave.

Even so, it tore him apart watching her. One more rejection. One more door slammed in her face. Once more out in the proverbial cold. They made one hell of a pair.

He scoured his face with his hands. All the while, The Inferno consumed him, raging with the urge to go to her. To fix this. To take her back into his arms and make her his again. His jaw tightened. The hell with it. This was just one more roadblock. A huge one, granted. But surely they could—

The front door opened and quietly closed, locking behind her. Sev charged into the living room, but she was gone, leaving nothing behind but a cold gleam emanating from the fireplace. Sitting on the hearth he found the engagement ring he'd given her. He crossed the room and picked it up.

Maybe it was his imagination, but he could have sworn the fire deep within the heart of the diamond had dimmed.

Francesca sat at her drawing board in her New York office, an office not that dissimilar from the one she'd occupied in San Francisco. Exhaustion dogged her, thanks to an endless round of sleepless nights. She'd only been in New York for a month, but already it felt like a lifetime. She rubbed her eyes, struggling to get them to focus on designs that could only be described as mediocre, at best. For some reason, her heart wasn't in her work anymore.

But then, how could it be? The past few weeks had been some of the darkest and most difficult of her life, far worse than anything she'd gone through in foster care. Worse even than her father's rejection. She'd made a hideous mistake when she'd contacted Bloom's rep.

Why hadn't it occurred to her that by helping the Fontaines, she was betraying Dantes . . . and more specifically, the man she loved? She'd been so busy easing her own guilt over leaving TH, that she never gave a thought to how her decision would impact Sev. Or that thanks to their feelings for each other, he wouldn't see her actions from a business standpoint, but take her betrayal personally. She'd simply reacted to what she'd perceived as an unfair situation, and taken matters into her own hands.

That still didn't explain why he hadn't acknowledged the designs she'd given him on their last night together. She'd hoped he'd understand what they meant. Hoped he'd realize that while she'd won the Bloom account for TH, she'd left him something far more valuable.

A familiar longing filled her as The Inferno gave her a small, petulant kick. Even after all this time the connection remained—stretched thin and taut, granted. Yet, it held with unbelievable tenacity.

The phone on her desk let out a shrill ring and she picked it up, surprised to have her greeting answered with a cheerful, *"Ciao, sorella.* It's Marco."

Pleasure mingled with disappointment at the sound of his voice. Pleasure to hear from a Dante. And disappointment that it wasn't the right Dante. "It's good to hear from you," she replied. "Though I'm surprised that any of you are willing to talk to me."

"You'd be even more surprised by how many of us are on your side." He hesitated. "I'm afraid I can't talk right now. I actually called to ask about some missing designs. Sev would like to know what happened to them. They're not in your old office. I don't suppose you took them with you to New York?"

She frowned. "I don't understand. I gave them to Sev."

"When, Francesca?"

"The night—" She broke off. The night they'd last made love. "The night before I transferred to New York. I brought them to Sev's apartment."

"He claims he doesn't have them."

Memory kicked in. "It had been raining the night I gave him the designs and I was soaked through. I vaguely recall he took them and tossed them onto the floor, out of the way." An image flashed through her mind. "I think they slid under that lovely old armoire he has in the entryway. You know the one I mean? He may not have noticed."

"Got it. Thanks, Francesca." He hesitated. "Are you . . . are you doing okay?"

No. Not even close to okay. "I'm fine."

"Right." She could hear the irony slipping through the line. "About as fine as Sev, I'd guess."

Francesca closed her eyes. "I have to be fine," she whispered. "We both do. There isn't any other choice."

"You didn't need to come with me," Sev informed Marco. "I'm perfectly capable of looking under my own coat closet."

"I came to try and make you see sense, as you damn well know."

"I always see sense. I'm the most sensible

of the lot of you."

"Not about this. Not when it comes to Francesca."

Sev shoved his key into the front door lock and twisted so hard it was a wonder the metal didn't snap off in his hand. "What's gotten into you, Marco? What part of *she betrayed us* don't you get?"

"And how many times did you betray her?" his brother shot back. "I know. I know. You had valid reasons. It was all about protecting Dantes. So, answer me this, hotshot. What makes that okay and what she did not okay? She was protecting her family the same as you."

That very question had been tearing Sev apart. How could he explain to his brother that it wasn't about business anymore? How could he explain the irrational belief that this betrayal felt personal? That this time he'd allowed his emotions to override his common sense? For the first time in his life, he, the Dante who prided himself on cool, emotionless deliberation, who used calm logic and rational thinking to govern all of his business decisions, hadn't been able to utilize any of his skills or abilities.

When it came to Francesca he was neither emotionless, nor logical, let alone cool and calm. The very thought of her caused a burning desire so overwhelming it didn't leave room for anything else.

Marco followed Sev into the apartment. Stooping, he reached under the coat closet and snagged a large, thick envelope. "Here it is. Right where she said it'd be." He sent the packet spinning in Sev's direction. "Happy now? Glad you didn't accuse her of selling her designs to the competition?"

Sev jerked as though punched. "She'd never—" he said automatically.

"You're right. She'd never." Marco glared at him. "Do you have any idea how lucky you are? Do you have any idea what the rest of us would give to feel The Inferno for a woman like Francesca? To know we could actually share a life with a woman like her, instead of longing for what we can never have? Instead of settling for second best? I never thought I'd say this to you, of all people, but you're an ass, Severo Dante."

Without a word, Sev ripped open the envelope and pulled out a sketchpad. He flipped it open and spared it a swift glance. And then he froze. "Marco . . ."

"What now?" He shifted to stand beside Sev and whistled softly. "If you needed proof how much she loves you, here it is."

Sev nodded. Page after page revealed some of the most incredible jewelry designs he'd ever seen. Designs ideal for the expansion Dantes' planned for some point in the future. It didn't take much thought to understand what she'd done.

Or why.

He understood all too well why she'd left these designs, designs she'd clearly been working on for years. She'd taken with one hand by giving the Bloom account to TH, and given with the other by presenting Dantes with these designs, dispensing a rough sort of justice. Only, she had more than compensated Dantes for what she'd given to Timeless Heirlooms.

She'd left him an incomparable gift, one that decimated the priorities he'd set in stone the day he'd first taken over from his father. A gift that made him realize there could only be one priority in his life from this point forward, and it wasn't Dantes.

The gift she'd given him wasn't the designs contained in her sketchpad. She'd left behind the gift of her heart.

Another month passed after Francesca's conversation with Marco. A month of pain and sorrow and regret. During those weeks, she'd come to the realization that Sev's feelings for her were truly dead, that The Inferno no longer burned for him the way it still burned for her.

Even when she received instructions to return to San Francisco on company business, she'd been unable to summon so much as a spark of hope. After all, miracles didn't exist. She'd learned that at the tender of age of eight when she'd been discarded by the people she'd hoped would one day be her adoptive parents. She knew better than to expect the door to open and for her to be welcomed in. She'd been disappointed too many times. And Sev had made himself abundantly clear before sending her to New York. She no longer belonged to the Dante inner circle.

She crossed to the mirror and examined her dress. She'd been specifically asked by Sev's assistant to wear red in order to fit in with the theme chosen for this evening's festivities. What theme, no one had bothered to explain. So, Francesca picked the brightest, most glorious shade of red she could find.

The fitted bodice glittered with Swarovski crystal beads, while the chiffon skirt drifted outward from her hips to the floor in layers of handkerchief veils that lifted and swirled on an invisible breeze. After some debate, she chose to leave her hair down and it fell in heavy curls to shoulders bared by the halter neckline of the gown.

Dantes had sent over jewelry to wear for the evening. She'd never seen the pieces before, but they were positively breathtaking. The necklace and earrings were simple confections, as romantic as they were elegant, featuring some of the most stunning fire diamonds she'd ever seen. Based on the design of the engagement ring she'd worn for far too brief a time, she would bet these latest items were Primo's creations, as well.

After checking the mirror a final time, she forced herself to leave the relative safety of the suite before Sev sent out a search party. Not giving herself a chance to reconsider, she took the elevator to the lobby and crossed to the steps leading to the ballroom. She hesitated at the threshold, searching for a friendly face. Instantly a hum of desire turned her insides molten. She didn't doubt the cause. Without any hesitation, she turned her head, keying in on Sev.

How could she ever have imagined The Inferno had finished with them, or her love would dwindle over time? The urge to go to him, to touch him, to have him possess her mouth, her body, her very soul, slammed through her. It grew so strong, she could do nothing more than obey the silent imperative. She took a half-dozen steps in Sev's direction before a sudden whisper of voices swelled, then faded, leaving behind a thunderous silence.

Her step faltered and she glanced around, only then realizing that while she wore flaming red, everyone else present was dressed in black and white. Only one other person also wore red, if only a scrap of the color. Sev's pocket handkerchief was a rich shade of ruby that stood out against his black suit and white dress shirt. Feeling painfully conspicuous, she held her head high and finished wending her way toward him.

She greeted him with a cool nod, while inside she thumbed with the hellish fires of desire. "Mr. Dante."

A small smile played about his mouth. "Ms. Sommers. If you'll come with me?"

He led the way to a small dais and approached the microphone. "I'd like to thank everyone for coming this evening to Dantes' launch of a brand-new collection. With me is the creator of that collection, its heart and soul, Francesca Sommers."

She froze in total shock. More than anything she wanted to grab Sev's hand for support, to demand an explanation. She turned to look at him, and every thought slid from her head, except one. She still loved this man. Utterly. Totally. Completely. From this day until the end of days.

"What's going on?" she pleaded.

"Smile, sweetheart," he murmured. "They're all here for you."

"But . . . why?"

He stepped toward the microphone again. "Please enjoy your evening, as well as our grand launch of—" He swept his arms wide. *"Dante's Heart."*

From either side of the ballroom, models appeared, each wearing a different one of the designs Francesca had left behind for Sev to use. Designs she'd envisioned as a teenager. Designs she'd worked on for a full decade and never quite brought to life, until she'd opened her heart to love. To Sev's love. Only then had she found the spark that turned her creative flame into a creative inferno.

She began to tremble in reaction. "You're using my designs to relaunch Dantes into a full line of jewelry?" Why had he done this? What did it mean?

"Jewelry for the contemporary woman." His hands settled on her shoulders and he gazed down at her with eyes more vivid than the sun. "You're Dante's Heart, my love. At least you're this Dante's heart."

Applause exploded around them and excited chatter swelled as the assembled guests got their first look at the new line. Tears filled Francesca's eyes. "I love you, Sev. More than you can possibly guess. I'm sorry, so sorry for everything—"

He stopped her words with a shake of his head. "Don't apologize. That's for me to do. I never should have put you in such an impossible position. It won't happen again. From now on you are, and always will be, first in my life." He inclined his head toward the gathering. "Do you hear them, sweetheart?"

She said the first thing that popped into her head. "They're clapping."

He grinned. "How could they not? They're witnessing something extraordinary." He laced his hand with hers and something deep inside gave way, a rending of barriers that had been erected when she'd been a frightened child of five. And in its place, the connection between them expanded and grew, rooting deep and permanent. "Come with me. We need to talk."

She glanced toward the doors leading onto the balcony. "I think I know the perfect location."

Together they left the dais, intent only on escape. Not that they were allowed such an easy out. Family came first, as Primo enveloped her in a huge bear hug, followed by a warm embrace from Nonna. Marco approached, sweeping her into a dizzying dip and laughing kiss full on the mouth. Then Lazz, who settled for a chaste peck on the cheek. And finally, Nicolò, who kissed the back of her hand with old-world gallantry.

Next, friends and associates impeded their progress, raving about the collection and using words that left Francesca choked with emotion. Words like "spectacular" and "unparalleled" and "generation defining." Mere feet from escape, Francesca came face-to-face with the Fontaines.

Instantly, Sev's arm wrapped around her, offering strength and protection. She gave his hand a reassuring squeeze, an unspoken message that even though she appreciated his support, she intended to handle this confrontation on her own terms.

"Tina, Kurt." She offered a smile. Not one of apology. Not one of nervousness or regret. But an open smile of genuine affection. A smile from the heart.

To her astonishment, they responded in kind. "Has Severo told you the news?" Tina asked.

Francesca glanced in bewilderment from Sev back to the Fontaines. "What news?"

Sev shook his head. "I was hoping we'd run into you, so you could tell her, yourself."

Tina grinned. "We reached a compromise. Timeless Heirlooms is now a subsidiary of Dantes. But Sev's agreed that we can continue to run it, with a few changes to assist the bottom line."

"Such as Dantes being in charge of acquiring new designers," Sev inserted. "And a few fiscal repairs that Kurt will oversee."

Tina waved that aside. "With Dantes' name behind us and our contract with Juliet Bloom, TH is guaranteed to skyrocket to the top." Ever the businesswoman, she added, "Anytime you want to contribute one of your designs, my dear, you're more than welcome."

Sev gave Tina a pointed look. "I believe there's something else you wanted to tell Francesca."

Tina squirmed. "Oh, right. That." She released a gusty sigh. "I owe you an apology. Sev didn't tell me about your connection to Kurt. His PI did. The man tried to double his profit by reselling the information."

"I've since taken care of the matter," Sev added.

The tone of his voice left little doubt in Francesca's mind that the PI was bitterly regretting his most recent business decision. "Thank you for clearing that up," she said.

A nervous light appeared in Kurt's soft-blue eyes. "We were wondering . . . That is, Tina and I were wondering . . . Perhaps you'd be available some evening for dinner. I'd like the opportunity to get to know my daughter. If you're willing, that is." He visibly braced himself. "After all we've put you through, I'll understand if you'd rather not."

Francesca could feel her face crumpling and knew she teetered on the edge of totally losing it. Only Sev's presence at her back gave her the necessary strength to respond. "I'd like that. I'd like that very much," she managed to get out, praying they didn't hear the tears sprinkled through the words.

Tina broke from her husband's side and gave Francesca a swift hug. "I never wanted children. It's a messy business, one that never suited me. But having a grown stepdaughter sort of appeals. We can, I don't know, do lunch, or something. Shop and have drinks. Or if you'd prefer a more traditional stepmother, I can have you sweep out the hearth and fix me tea and dress you in soot-covered rags."

Francesca grinned through her tears at the Cinderella reference. "Works for me. The first part, I mean. Not the rest."

"Well, then. Fine." Tina cleared her throat, more awkward than Francesca had ever seen her. "We're all good, right?"

Francesca laughed. "Very good."

The instant the Fontaines departed, Sev cupped her elbow and urged her through the double doors and onto the balcony. The night held an unseasonable warmth, soft and balmy. Together they wandered to the balustrade and leaned against it. From their Nob Hill perch they could stare out at the bright lights that glittered below them like a carpet of diamond shards.

"This is where I first saw you," Francesca murmured.

"This is where I first fell in love with you." He turned to face her. "I'm sorry, Francesca. I should have trusted my instincts from the beginning. Hell, I should have trusted you. For most of my adult life it's been my job to protect my family and our business from all threats."

"And you saw me as a threat." Not much question about that.

"The biggest threat, because you were the one person capable of tempting me to forget honor and duty and responsibility."

"I'd never ask that of you," she protested. "All I've ever wanted is for you to open your heart and let me in."

"It's wide open, love, and just waiting for you to step across the threshold."

"Is that The Inferno talking?"

"Maybe it is. Or maybe The Inferno knows what lies in our hearts and forces stubborn men to see the truth. Because the truth is you're my heart and soul, and always will be. But I'd also like you to be my wife."

All her life she believed herself on the outside, looking in. Now she realized it wasn't true. It had never been true. Fear kept her from taking that final step, from seeing the open doors. They'd always been there, she'd just been too busy protecting herself from hurt to take that leap of faith and walk inside.

She took the step now, hurtling herself against Sev. His arms closed around her, bringing her home. And then he kissed her, telling her without words just how much he loved her. Long minutes passed before they drew apart.

He reached into his pocket and removed a familiar looking jeweler's box, emblazoned with the Dantes' logo. He thumbed it open, revealing a set of rings. The first was the engagement ring Primo designed, the other the band that mated with it. Maybe it was his imagination, but the fire diamond no longer appeared dim. Now it seemed to rage with its own inner inferno.

He slipped the engagement ring on her finger. "Will you marry me, Francesca, for real this time?"

She positively glowed. "Yes, yes, *yes!*"

And then he kissed her again, soothing old hurts and offering a promise for the future. Much, much later Francesca rested her head against Sev's shoulder, her happiness a palpable presence. She gazed toward the ballroom, misty-eyed, and then stiffened within his arms. "Sev, look."

He glanced in the direction she pointed and shrugged. "It's Marco. So what?"

"Look what he's doing with his hands."

Sev stared, his eyes narrowing when he saw it. Marco was busy entertaining a guest with one of his stories, and as he talked he dug the fingers of his left hand into the palm of his right. It could only mean one thing. Sometime, someplace . . .

"My God," he murmured. "Marco's been struck by The Inferno."

The Dante Inferno continues with
Marco's story!

Marco's Stolen Wife by Day Leclaire

Meet Day Leclaire

I love family first and foremost, which is why writing a family saga is so much fun. Maybe you can tell that from my books since they always feature the warmth and joy that comes from having a close-knit family. I also love animals and have taken in rescue dogs and cats and fostered dogs for the local animal shelter. And of course, I love writing. All I need is a functioning brain (batteries not included), a pen, and paper, and I can write anywhere. Please don't let a conversation with me lag because my imagination takes over and I. Am. Checked. Out!

USA Today bestselling author, Day Leclaire is the author of more than 60 novels and has received an impressive eleven nominations for the romance industry's most prestigious award, Romance Writers of America RITA© Award. Day lives in Charlotte, NC and spends her days obsessively writing while vaguely remembering to pay attention to her adorable husband, busy son and daughter-in-law, two tiny grandchildren, and two even tinier Teddy Bear dogs. Not to mention a whole lot of dust!

Thank you so much for taking the time to read **The Dante Inferno:** *The Dante Dynasty Series*. I hope you enjoy this very special Italian-American family. I love hearing from my readers. For a personal response, please contact me at Day@DayLeclaire.com. And be sure to visit my website at www.DayLeclaire.com. Sign up for my newsletter for my latest releases and insider info available nowhere else! Just visit: https://www.dayleclaire.com/join-my-mailing-list

You can also find me on Facebook at www.facebook.com/Day.Leclaire.Private and Twitter at www.Twitter.com/DayLeclaire.